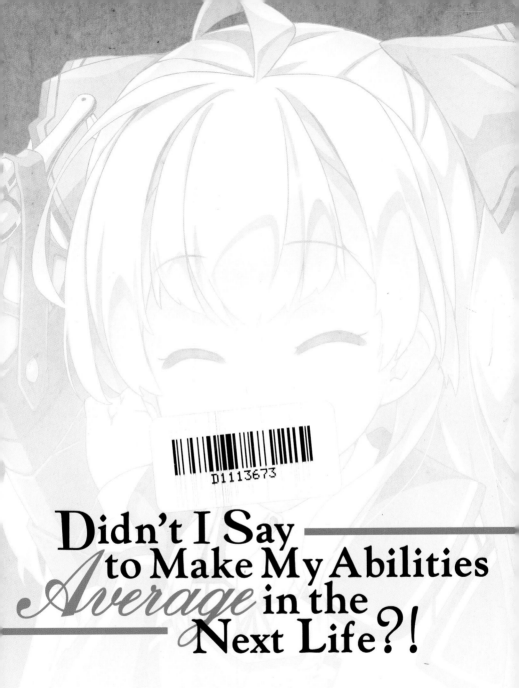

D1113673

Didn't I Say to Make My Abilities Average in the Next Life?!

VOLUME 4

Didn't I Say to Make My Abilities *Average* in the Next Life?!

DIDN'T I SAY TO MAKE MY ABILITIES AVERAGE
IN THE NEXT LIFE?! VOLUME 4

© FUNA / Itsuki Akata 2017

Originally published in Japan in 2017 by EARTH STAR
Entertainment, Tokyo. English translation rights arranged
with EARTH STAR Entertainment, Tokyo, through TOHAN
CORPORATION, Tokyo.

TRANSLATION: Diana Taylor
ADAPTATION: Michelle Danner-Groves
COVER DESIGN: Nicky Lim
INTERIOR LAYOUT & DESIGN: Clay Gardner
PROOFREADER: Jade Gardner, Dayna Abel
ASSISTANT EDITOR: Jenn Grunigen
LIGHT NOVEL EDITOR: Nibedita Sen
DIGITAL MANAGER: CK Russell
PRODUCTION DESIGNER: Lissa Pattillo
EDITOR-IN-CHIEF: Adam Arnold
PUBLISHER: Jason DeAngelis

ISBN:978-1-626929-37-1
Printed in Canada
First Printing: November 2018
10 9 8 7 6 5 4 3 2 1

Didn't I Say to Make My Abilities *Average* in the Next Life?!

VOLUME 4

BY

FUNA

ILLUSTRATED BY

Itsuki Akata

Seven Seas Entertainment

God bless me?

CONTENTS

CHAPTER 27:	SIXTEEN YEARS SINCE...	15
CHAPTER 28:	A SORTIE	27
CHAPTER 29:	DEMONIC DEEDS	63
CHAPTER 30:	A FEARSOME FIGHT! THE SUNRISE BATTLE	79
CHAPTER 31:	TO THE CAPITAL	107
CHAPTER 32:	ONCE MORE INTO THE FOREST	117
CHAPTER 33:	FIGHT TO THE FINISH	147
CHAPTER 34:	A BATTLE OF MAGIC	163
CHAPTER 35:	THE RUINS	181
CHAPTER 36:	WORRIES	203
CHAPTER 37:	DECISIONS	227
CHAPTER 38:	THE START OF A NEW JOURNEY	241
SIDE STORY:	MARCELA'S TUG-OF-WAR	253
BONUS STORY:	RANKINGS	275
	AFTERWORD	279

The Kingdom of Tils

Mile

A girl who was granted "average" abilities in this fantasy world.

Reina

A rookie hunter. Specializes in combat magic.

Pauline

A rookie hunter. A timid girl, however...

Mavis

A swordswoman. Leader of the up-and-coming party, the Crimson Vow.

The Kingdom of Brandel

Marcela

Adele's friend. A magic user of noble birth.

Morena

The king's third daughter. Intrigued by Adele.

Lenny

A girl at the inn. Passionate about money.

Veil

A rookie hunter from the Hunters' Prep School. Looks after the orphans in the slums.

$\mathcal{P}reviously$

When Adele von Ascham, the eldest daughter of Viscount Ascham, was ten years old, she was struck with a terrible headache and just like that, remembered everything.

She remembered how, in her previous life, she was an eighteen-year-old Japanese girl named Kurihara Misato who died while trying to save a young girl, and that she met God...

Misato had exceptional abilities, and the expectations of the people around her were high. As a result, she could never live her life the way she wanted. So when she met God, she made an impassioned plea:

"In my next life, please make my abilities average!"

Yet somehow, it all went awry.

In her new life, she can talk to nanomachines and, although her magical powers are technically average, it is the average between a human's and an elder dragon's...6,800 times that of a sorcerer!

At the first academy she attended, she made friends and rescued a little boy as well as a princess. She registered at the Hunters' Prep School under the name of Mile, and at the graduation exam went head-to-head with an A-rank hunter.

A lot has happened, but now Mile is going to live a normal life as a rookie hunter with her allies by her side.

Because she is a perfectly normal, *average* girl!

CHAPTER 27

Sixteen Years Since...

IT HAD BEEN SIXTEEN YEARS since the day Reina first opened her eyes.

Yes, Reina was sixteen years old.

Mavis, at seventeen, was currently the oldest in their group. Reina, at sixteen, was a close second. Then came Pauline at fifteen and finally Mile, who was only thirteen. Oh, and it would be Mavis's birthday very soon.

With Pauline finally fifteen, Mile was now the only member of the Crimson Vow who was still underage.

However, as one could become a full member of the Hunters' Guild at ten years of age and this country did not have age restrictions on things like voting and drinking alcohol, it made very little difference if one had achieved the official age of adulthood (fifteen years) or not.

The more important distinction here—whether in terms of employment, legal matters, or parental responsibility—was whether or not one had turned ten. That was the age at which children normally began trying to make an honest living instead of just pocket money, although most of them, other than hunters, would find employment only as apprentices and errand boys and not earn very much at all.

Marcela and the others will be third years now, Mile thought. *I wonder if Crooktail and the others are doing well...*

As far as Mile was concerned, all of her former classmates ranked lower than the cat. Only the Wonder Trio really mattered to her.

And I'm thirteen now. Huh. I have an early birthday, so the rest of them are probably still twelve. Come to think of it, if I were still in Japan, I would be in my second year of junior high now.

That's the year when people are supposed to contract junior high syndrome—the adolescent arrogance they call chuunibyou. *But that has nothing to do with me anymore.*

After all, I have the strength of a dragon, immense magical powers, and mysterious little creatures only I can see who can answer my every inquiry. And memories...of my...past life...

Mile collapsed onto her bed.

"There've been a lot of weird requests lately," Reina muttered, standing before the guild's job board.

In addition to the typical gathering quests, extermination orders, and escort duties, there were investigation-type jobs posted.

Investigating monsters in the mountains.

Investigating why monsters that usually stayed deep in the forest had begun appearing around towns and villages.

Searching for parties that had gone missing, with additional rewards for rescuing them, uncovering the reason for their disappearances, retrieving the belongings of the deceased, and so on.

Several of the investigation jobs, including requests for culling and eliminating fairly high-ranked monsters that came near human settlements, seemed to converge on a single town.

"The town of Helmont? Why does that sound familiar?" Mile asked.

"Because we just went there to capture the wyvern!" Reina replied.

"Oh right, the Mysterious Bird, Lobreth!"

As Mile patted her fist on her palm in recognition, Mavis muttered, "We keep telling you, a wyvern isn't a bird."

"Hmm, all the jobs around here are pretty normal. They pay well enough, but they're kind of boring."

Mavis and Pauline, having heard such from Reina before, hurriedly looked around. In truth, they felt the same way. However, they were in the middle of a guildhall, surrounded by hunters who were doing their best to earn a daily living. Saying things such as "These jobs are all so normal it's boring," or "I guess they pay well enough," was unacceptable. They were sure to stir up trouble.

After all, not everyone had above average mages and swordsmen in their group or possessed absurd amounts of magic. Hardly anyone ever earned as much as they did on normal gathering or extermination requests.

Reina soon realized this and managed to look embarrassed. Thankfully, none of the other hunters had heard her, or at least no one seemed to be looking their way. The four of them breathed a sigh of relief.

"A-anyway, these must be pretty unpopular requests, getting recirculated all the way to the capital," said Reina before hurriedly correcting herself. "Taking care of these jobs would earn us a lot of brownie points with the guild!"

Yes, that phrasing was unlikely to ruffle any feathers.

As far as the other hunters and the guild were concerned, having a skilled young party taking leftover jobs even veterans weren't interested in—that weren't even worth their pay—was a good thing. It increased the prestige of the capital guild branch.

Of course, when it came to their true motives, any young man or woman would grow dissatisfied with taking on boring, normal jobs just to earn a living. For middle-aged hunters with spouses and children, work was nothing more than a means of supporting their families. Young hunters found it far easier to convince themselves that "I want to do a huge job!" or "I want to promote my name!"

So, naturally, the Crimson Vow—which included Reina, aiming for a B-rank, and Mavis, who dreamed of becoming an A-rank and enlisting as a knight—had similar inclinations.

Well, perhaps that wasn't quite the right way to put it. Mile and Pauline had little interest in such things, and even as young hunters went, Mavis and Reina's desires for promotion weren't especially strong.

The Crimson Vow were relieved, assuming no one else had heard Reina's words. But of course, that wasn't *actually* the case. The guildhall wasn't especially large, so four notable rookie hunters—who happened to also be cute girls—standing around making a fuss attracted attention. Plus, their high-pitched voices carried far.

Everyone was just pretending they hadn't heard them.

What would the rookies do about troublesome, suspicious jobs even veterans considered unworthy of their time? What fascinating tale would they hear from the girls who not only succeeded at the wyvern-hunting job—considered a "red mark," a job that would see "the red blood of their allies flowing and put red marks upon their records"—but had done it without a scratch?

The hunters and employees of the capital branch of the Hunters' Guild listened with rapt attention, gazes averted, pretending they didn't care.

"So, which one should we do?"

As Reina ruminated, Mile pointed to one of the postings.

"Reina, look here..."

"*Special value pack! Upon accepting the task to settle matters in Helmont, hunters may take on only as many tasks as they feel up to handling, at any time, with no fees or penalties for non-completion or failure. Wages paid in proportion to job success.*"

"Wh-what is this?! This is the first time I've ever seen a posting with such convenient terms!"

"Doesn't that just mean no one is around to take the jobs? Or that the danger is great in proportion to the pay, or that the failure rate is high?" asked Pauline.

"Yeah," Mavis agreed, "No mistaking that. Plus, they're probably looking to get several parties involved at once."

"This is another one of *those*, isn't it? What Laylia was talking about before."

"Yeah, a 'red mark' job, right? Red, like the color of the blood that will flow or the 'red mark' upon your record... But, even so!"

"We'll be taking this special 'red mark' job!" the four announced in unison.

Hearing this, Laylia, the receptionist, shrugged her shoulders. Her face fell in a way that perfectly indicated she had given up on life.

Mile, seeing the words "special value pack," suddenly felt rather unsettled.

I wonder if that comes with fries...

"You all again?"

It was six days later.

When they arrived again in Helmont, the Crimson Vow stopped in to see the guild master, who had previously explained the wyvern situation to them.

"Well, thanks to that last job, I have a good idea of what you can do. However, this job might be more dangerous than that one. Several parties have already failed to return and have been registered as missing. I won't say more, but you'd best leave this one alone. There're plenty of other jobs to take, and no matter how skilled you are, it's not smart to take on troublesome, dangerous jobs while you're still lacking in experience. You should take jobs like this after you've had more time to grow. You're still young—there's no need to rush."

The guild master wasn't belittling the Crimson Vow, but rather, admonishing them out of genuine concern.

"Even so," Reina replied, "We already accepted the job in the capital."

"No," the guild master said. "You may have taken on the job in the capital, but it originated here. If I personally judge that 'the job candidates are unsuitable,' then the contract can be dissolved. You haven't failed in any way, so you won't take any penalties, and we'll cover your travel expenses from and to the capital, as well as the breach of contract fee.

"What do you think? If that sounds good to you, we can go ahead and do that."

The guild master's proposal came from a place of kindness. If they accepted, it would mean taking losses on the guild's part, with no profit gained. Simply leaving things as they were, on the other hand, wouldn't cost the guild a single copper, as the payment for the job would have already been set aside.

It was a proposal made for the sake of the girls, at the cost of the guild.

However, the way the guild master suggested they give up

gave the girls a bad feeling. Though he encouraged them to give up, in truth, the four of them got the feeling he was simply hesitant to refuse them.

But then:

Reina offered a stern refusal. "We decline. If we intended to give up after coming this far," she explained, "we wouldn't have taken the job in the first place. We agreed with full awareness of the pros and cons, so do you really think we'd simply roll over because someone asked us to? Plus, why would 'it's dangerous' give us pause?"

Seeing the other three nodding in agreement, a crestfallen but oddly hopeful look briefly crossed the guild master's face. However, it vanished in an instant. The guild master's stoic visage returned.

"Don't overdo it. The moment you feel you are in danger, abandon the investigation and return here. That is my stipulation as your employer, which you cannot refuse. If that's no good for you, then you better give up now. Got it?"

The guild master's face and voice were serious, but the Crimson Vow weren't so dense as to miss his true meaning. They nodded in agreement.

"Well, you really did help us out with that wyvern. Thanks to you, even our lord has finally come to recognize what hunters bring to the table and now seems a bit more favorable toward the guild. So we really have to thank you for that.

"I guess I better fill you in. You can find more details about each individual job down on the first floor. First off, starting a short while ago, monster sightings in the forest and the mountains have become rarer. Monsters you would normally be able to find without trouble have vanished, and monsters that never used to reside here have started to appear. Numerous hunting parties have been injured. There are groups who haven't returned at all and are likely..."

A dark look spread across the man's face. In other words, *something* had probably befallen those hunters.

"Are those the parties we would be searching for?" Mavis asked.

He shook his head.

"No. If a hunter is injured or lost while on a job or out harvesting, that's their own responsibility. Only people who take jobs where they're out of their depth should be at risk. The guild doesn't go out of its way to search for such folks, although their family and other close acquaintances will occasionally put up money to list it as an official request.

"The ones you'll be searching for are part of an official guild investigation team. They're comprised of veteran hunters, knowledgeable about the forest and its monsters; two scholars; and a guild employee who went along as an escort."

This guild employee, they soon found out, had some measure of magical ability.

Even if she could only use a middling amount of generalized magic, having her along when there were non-hunters involved could be a huge help. Non-hunters often made selfish demands, but such problems were usually quickly neutralized when magic-users were there. Plus, it was helpful to know, on the off chance something went awry, that they wouldn't have to worry about simple but important things like finding water.

If the employee in question was a young woman, the men also wouldn't have any objection to her accompanying them. No, not in the slightest.

The guild master outlined the investigation team's plan, the items they had intended to investigate, and the monsters they would like culled if the chance arose. They would be able to confirm the rest of the details and receive maps and materials from the receptionist on the first floor, later.

As the four of them stood from their seats to leave, the guild master called out to them.

"The guild employee who went along with the investigation team..."

The girls stopped and turned to face him. He continued.

"She's... she's my daughter. So... please."

To save his daughter, he wanted someone, *anyone*, to take the job and search for her. Even if the worst had come to pass, he wanted someone to confirm her passing and bring back her body. Or at least some memento of her.

The guild master spoke with conflicting emotions: the grief and desperation of a father, clutching at whatever hope he had; and the duty of a guild master, unwilling to send young hunters off to needless death.

They understood how he felt. The four gave the guild master, whose head was bowed, a thumbs-up.

"We will absolutely—" said Mavis.

"Make your wish come true!" they chimed in unison.

Of course, this happened to be a line they had rehearsed ahead of time for just such an event.

Thankfully, like in Japan and most English-speaking areas of Earth, a thumbs-up indicated a positive response in this country. However, it was always important to use such gestures with care, as they *could* be offensive in certain regions and countries. Indeed, there were some places where the white flag was the call for a battle to the death, not a cease-fire.

Leaving the guild master behind them, the four girls departed.

The guild master's daughter had volunteered to escort the investigation team, thinking that the only other woman on the team—a young female student—might be lonely if she was the only girl out there. Or so the guild master had said before revealing the employee was his daughter.

She had taken a big risk, but they would do her best to save her. She was worth it.

Besides, if all good women died young, the world would be a much more boring place.

With that in mind, the Crimson Vow swore to avoid dying young themselves, of course.

CHAPTER 28 |

A Sortie

THE NEXT DAY...

"You all ready? Let's go!"

"Yeah!"

And so, the Crimson Vow set out.

It was half a day's journey to the village where they had captured Lobreth. The area was deep in the forest, but the villagers
took quite a bit of offense to that description. They preferred to
think their home was "a village on the outskirts of the forest."

The going was easy, so the group reached the borders of the
village before noon. They knew, however, not to stop in the town;
the welcoming committee would hold them up. So, the girls
passed through without stopping. The fact that they didn't need
to replenish their water supply worked out in their favor.

Soon, they passed through what the villagers referred to as
"the true entrance of the forest."

Just as they entered this neck of the woods and thought to themselves, *Why, this is no different from any other part of the forest*—a fangbear suddenly appeared. It was a strange beast to encounter here: more powerful than most regular creatures and clearly looking for easy prey. It was like they were in an RPG and had suddenly encountered a mid-level boss the moment they left the "Starting Village."

Well, that was unfortunate for the fangbear. The Crimson Vow wasn't a group of Level 1 onion knights equipped with wooden rods, but rather a group of garlic knights equipped with fearsome mystery blades.

Eep!

"It's pretty dangerous to have something like this hanging around where the forest is still so thin," Pauline observed.

After processing and storing away the fangbear, they proceeded deeper into the forest.

"It seems like there are a lot of small animals too... I guess they ran away from the heart of the woods."

Just as Pauline said, there were many more animals and monsters around than usual. They hunted anything that would threaten the village as they traveled, along with the monsters the guild had instructed them to catch or cull. Mile stored them in her inventory, feigning storage magic as usual.

It was mostly for their own peace of mind, but the hunting was good to do. Besides, it was part of their job description. They could sell parts for an added reward on top of their commission, as well. Of course, finding the investigation team in a timely manner was their priority, so the party moved along, hunting only when it wouldn't slow down their progress.

Darkness came early in the forest. It had been around midday when they first entered the woods, so they decided to make camp once it was too dark for them to go further safely.

Tomorrow, they would set out as soon as it was light. They ate a light dinner and headed immediately to bed.

"Something is a little strange here," said Reina.

Indeed, as they continued toward the heart of the forest on the second day, something felt off. This was the first time the girls had entered this part of the forest, so the only information they had to go off of was what people had told them. However, compared to other forests, something was clearly strange here.

First off, it was lacking the animals and monsters that had been abnormally numerous on the first day. There were very few of the mid-sized beasts around as well, perhaps because the field mice, jackalopes, and other small creatures they usually fed on were scarce.

By contrast, fangbears, ogres, and other fairly strong monsters were numerous. Since these were among the creatures the guild had asked them to thin out, the Crimson Vow felled one after another. Mile put them away with her "storage magic" (read: inventory).

Normally, such prey would be impossible to transport, and hunters resorted to cutting off some token part as proof of the kill. The Crimson Vow weren't like other hunters, though. Their earning rates were in a league of their own.

They got the feeling that all the more hapless wildlife had been driven out, while only the stronger, more territorial creatures remained. Of course, many stronger creatures had moved out for the same reason or left in pursuit of the animals that were their prey.

Just like that very first fangbear they encountered.

"I can think of a number of reasons why we might not be seeing weaker animals and monsters here," Reina said. "Number one: their own food sources have vanished. Number two: the number of creatures that want to make *them* food has increased. Number three: it's become difficult for them to live here for some other reason. Or number four: a large number of them suddenly went extinct."

Answering the hand signs Reina made as she spoke with a subtle nod, Mile nonchalantly reached her left hand down and grasped the slingshot at her belt. Her right hand slipped into her pocket to grab a stone.

Whoosh!

Mile quickly slipped the pebble into the pouch and let it fly. The pebble soared through the air fruitlessly, disappearing into the trees.

"Sorry, I missed."

"That's fine. I'm sure it will come back again," Reina said.

Indeed, something had been peering down at the girls from a nearby tree. Unsure whether or not this something was a human, Mile had used a somewhat dialed-down attack, but it had been avoided.

Mile had become more skilled with her slingshot, so lately, not wanting to rely too much on the nanomachines, she had been forgoing their course correction. However, her aim was still true.

She hadn't missed; her target had dodged. In other words, this was proof that it had been looking directly their way.

"Anyway, we know that it isn't reason number one or two. All the grasses, fruits, and bugs the prey animals usually eat are normal, and we didn't see a large number of mid-sized animals or monsters either. Plus, I don't see signs of any great calamity or environmental change that would have caused a sudden mass extinction, so number four is out..."

"H-hey, Reina, just a minute ago, what was that?" Mavis asked.

Ignoring her, Reina continued as though nothing were out of the ordinary.

"In that case, we can assume this isn't because of natural causes, but rather the work of some external force. And if the makeup of the monsters in the area suddenly changed—"

Mile continued. "Then these stronger creatures either evolved or invaded, and caused a change in the local biosphere?"

Reina nodded. Mavis and Pauline's eyes went wide with shock.

"M-Mile," said Mavis, "You're using a lot of big words there, but do you understand what they all mean?"

Pauline nodded in agreement. Apparently, *that* was what the two were shocked about.

"Didn't I already tell you that I was head of the class back in my home country?!"

"Well, we thought that was because you crushed all the honor students with your magical skills."

"Whoever said it was anything like that?!?!"

"Layl—uh, no one. It was no one!"

"Laylia?! It was Miss Laylia, wasn't it?!"

"Waahhh..."

"Now, shall we continue our conversation?" Reina said, her voice strained as veins popped on her forehead.

The other three girls snapped to attention.

"Yes, ma'am!"

"So, I was thinking maybe something like a fenrir or an earth dragon appeared. If that's the case, then just confirming the existence of the creature will mean half of our job is done, but given the sense we've been getting..."

If such a monster were to appear, even a party of four A-rank hunters would be no match for it. The guild had already assumed a party of only a few hunters couldn't handle the task in the first place, which is why the job was an "investigation" and "finding the source." "Elimination" wasn't part of their mission. That would happen after the cause had been determined, and they had a chance to organize for battle. This was merely a preliminary investigation toward that end.

"Someone's watching us?" Naturally, Pauline had a sharp nose as far as such matters were concerned.

"Yeah, and given the fact that it was watching from above the trees, and that it disappeared in the blink of an eye, I don't get the feeling that it's a human we're dealing with," Reina said.

Mavis, who was normally quick to spot enemies, looked shocked. She hadn't noticed, but she had never been very good at detecting foes who intentionally obscured their presence.

Mile wasn't fond of using tricks, and was scared of everyone becoming too reliant on her, and so she had not been using her long-range detection magic. However, being negligent—or worse, letting them stumble into a situation they couldn't escape—was a scarier prospect, so she had been using short-range detection magic to at least ward off surprise attacks. That was how she had noticed the watcher, but the fact that Reina had done so without magic was even more impressive.

In reply to Reina's implication that the thing watching them was not human, the other three asked as one:

"...A demon?"

Yes, saying that something that "wasn't human" was in this forest immediately brought to mind what the elderly mage (naturally, they had all long since forgotten his name) had said about receiving his pet "from a demon."

Everyone's expressions went tense.

The Crimson Vow could brag that they were no longer rookies but proper C-rank hunters. But with a demon as their potential opponent, they were suddenly nervous. "Demons" were really just another race, the name of which came from a truncation of the phrase "decidedly magical persons." They couldn't assume that the individual in question was of lower-than-average ability.

Looking at this objectively, the only one with any possibility of winning a one-on-one battle with such a being was Mile, and even that was just a possibility.

If the four girls took on demons as opponents, they could reasonably handle two—assuming the demons were weaker than they imagined. They probably weren't. The demons in legends were always much stronger than anyone imagined.

Of course, legends only ever told of the most grandiose of events.

Indeed, just like Mile's "Japanese Folktales."

Unthinkingly, Mavis began to fiddle with her pockets. In them were two containers Mile had given her; two very small, metal containers. Mile had handed them to her before they left the capital, "in case of an emergency." Because they were small and metal, they would be difficult to break.

However, the Japanese folktale Mile had told them after giving her the containers was the one known as "A Slice of Bread." What was the significance of that?

Slightly, ever so slightly, Mavis glared at Mile.

The Crimson Vow proceeded through the forest for several more hours.

The path they followed was the investigation team's planned route, provided by the guild. The primary directive for this job was to search for the missing team, so they had little other choice but to keep to that plan.

The missing hunters had been free to follow whichever leads

they chose, but the Crimson Vow stuck to the route as much as possible. They had, after all, made a promise.

"We will absolutely... make your wish come true!"

They had no obligation to honor an oath coerced by threat or force. In fact, it was better to simply laugh off such oaths and put them firmly out of mind.

But promises made to people who believed in them? Promises made to people who were desperate or hurt? Those were the promises they simply couldn't break. No matter what happened.

Even if her chances of survival were painfully slim—even if all they could bring back was a piece of her or her belongings—the four of them would find the guild master's daughter, and bring her home. They had given him their solemn vow, and they would see it through with conviction.

"There's a lot fewer of them, aren't there?" said Mile.

"Yeah," Mavis agreed.

Just as the two noted, the numbers of the monsters they had been told to cull were shrinking.

That could only mean one thing.

"We're here! There's eight people, three hundred meters ahead!"

They had reached the source of whatever had caused the unusual relocation of the creatures in the forest.

"They don't look like monsters, like goblins or orcs. They look...like they're human..."

Mile's words were halting, but they understood. It was likely because the people were demons, and so her detection magic had a slightly different reaction than it did with humans. Coming to this conclusion, Reina couldn't contain herself.

"We have to launch a counterattack! Our enemies are probably stronger than us. When an enemy launches a surprise attack on you, you have to intercept them with your own counterattack. Consider this our only chance of winning."

These were rather pessimistic words, but if their opponents were even half as strong as the ones she remembered from her father's bedtime stories, or the ones she read about in fairy tales and legends, then their chances of victory were slim.

In the middle of the woods, they wouldn't be able to shake off a group of opponents who were well versed in the terrain and likely had far greater physical abilities than themselves. They would likely run themselves to exhaustion and then be pounced on, or picked off, one by one.

All they had managed so far was being stalked by demons and learning that the destruction they'd been seeing was possibly demon handiwork, but that did mean they had fulfilled the investigation portion of the job. Now, they needed to determine what sort of force would be necessary to get rid of the demons.

And then they had to make it home alive.

Whssh!

Suddenly, two shapes whizzed out of the treetops.

"Earth Rod!"

"Water Spear!"

Bang!

Ka-shunk!

One of the pair of enemies who had suddenly descended from the treetops toward Reina and Pauline, hoping to instantaneously disable the backline fighters, was struck hard by the rod of earth that Reina had conjured and tumbled to the ground. The other was struck by Pauline's water spear and crumpled in turn.

Because the attack was made of water, the spear didn't pierce the enemy's body; however, the force of the water compounded with the speed of descent increased the attack's power several fold.

"Huh...?"

The four stood perplexed. Thanks to Mile's precise detection magic, they had accurately predicted when their enemies would strike. However, they hadn't expected their attackers would be felled so easily, nor that they would attack physically rather than with magic.

However, just as they moved to observe the creatures crumpled on the ground...

"Don't move!"

They looked back only to see four enemies at their rear. The other two were probably hiding somewhere. Atop the heads of these enemies who had now shown their faces were...ears. Strange ears.

A pair of tall, pricked-up cat ears. Lopped and drooping dog ears. Fox ears. Rabbit ears.

And they all had fluffy tails.

"B-beastpeople?" the girls gasped in unison.

Indeed, no matter how you looked at them, they weren't human. But they weren't demons, either.

"Don't resist and you won't get hurt. Keep quiet and throw down your weapons."

If the beastpeople—or rather beastmen, now that they looked—had intended to kill them from the start, they would have been better off attacking with spears or bows, rather than plunging from the trees. Even now, with the Crimson Vow so off guard, they could have launched an attack without preamble.

That they did not meant that they probably only intended to capture them.

Even so, this didn't mean the Crimson Vow would just surrender and allow themselves to be captured. Regardless of the beastmen's apparent intentions, there was no guarantee that they wouldn't be interrogated or offered up as living sacrifices to some vengeful god.

Plus, they had yet to offer any reason as to why the girls should be detained in the first place.

Now that they knew that their opponents were not in fact demons, the Crimson Vow had a bit more room to work. Though beastpeople had greater physical prowess than humans, they lacked magic. This was probably why they had schemed to take the mages out from the start. Unfortunately, that plan had fallen apart.

It was likely they had made light of the Crimson Vow, thinking that with two little girls in the front and two novice mages at the rear—and all with the weak physicality of humans—they would be easily overtaken. Even now, the beastmen seemed to think that the two companions on the ground before them was just a side effect of their sneak attack.

"If you don't resist, we won't kill you. Lie down on the ground, bellies up," Reina commanded.

"Wh...?" The four beastmen were dumbfounded.

This was unthinkable. The position Reina demanded they assume was one of utter submission and absolutely humiliating. They would never do so willingly, and certainly not on the command of some little human girl.

Of course, there was no way someone as smart as Reina wasn't aware of this. She was clearly trying to provoke them.

Being taken prisoner in a place like this would be a problem, and of course, to simply do as they said would be unthinkable. So, they needed to wrap this up quickly—in other words, by goading them into battle. That way they could say that their enemies had attacked them and they had merely responded with "justified self-defense."

However, this gambit wasn't something Reina had concocted independently. It was one of several that the four had planned ahead of time for just such a situation, having brainstormed many such scenarios they might encounter on the job.

Naturally, they did not intend to kill them. This was a plan concocted with a great deal of thought. The moment she realized their opponents weren't demons, Reina had decided to act on it.

"Y-you little... Looks like this little lady's underestimating us,"

The four beastmen approached, spitting the phrase the girls had now heard so many times before. They were equipped not with swords but with something more like machetes. These were perhaps not originally intended as weapons but as tools for navigating through the woods.

First off, Mile was clearly much stronger than these men.

And, if Mavis strengthened her resolve and went into 'True Godspeed Blade' mode, they shouldn't be any problem for her either.

And while Pauline and Reina defended themselves with their staves and their spells would be less powerful than usual, they were accustomed to firing off quickly incanted spells, which would give them the advantage in battle. With enough leeway, they could probably even let off a slightly more powerful spell. Plus, they had already silently prepared their first spells, just waiting to let them off.

Mile would have sensed where the two hidden enemies were by now, so they were no problem, either.

With this all in mind, Reina thrust out her left hand, palm to the sky, middle finger beckoning.

Yes, this gesture was a sign of provocation: *Bring it.*

"Y-you little... All right then, let's go! Just be careful not to kill them!"

Apparently, the beastmen really didn't intend to harm them. At least, not here. But now they were in combat, so all bets were off.

They might not want to kill the Crimson Vow, but on the field, with both sides swinging their weapons around, who knew what might happen? Even if they actively tried to avoid vital areas, they might still land a fatal blow while dodging an enemy attack, or something like that. Such things happened often.

Before the four beastmen rushed them, the two who had been lying in wait sprung out from the opposite side. It was a clever tactic, designed to invite more chaos than leaping out at the same time as the rest of the attackers. It was very much a ploy of those used to close-range combat.

Inexperienced opponents would be flummoxed by such a tactic. Unsettled, startled. The Crimson Vow? *Not so much.*

They faced the attackers coming at them from the front, Mile and Mavis taking one apiece. The other two men ignored them and aimed for the mages on the backline. Reina and Pauline met them with fire magic and ice magic in turn.

Reina—certain they would assume the girls were too distraught to make a move, given that they did not appear to be casting any spell, and so would be close enough that no attack would miss—had silently prepped a flame ball with her fire magic and let it fly into one attacker's gut. Likewise, the other took Pauline's ice spear. Both were blown backwards.

The tip of Pauline's ice spear was blunted, so the beastman who took her attack wasn't gravely injured. Reina's attacker's injuries were more severe, his stomach covered with harsh burns. These beastmen wore neither metal nor leather armor, or even simple leather guards.

...Apparently, beastpeople relied a little too much on their pelts.

Mile blocked the swing of her opponent's machete before swinging her own sword. She knocked the weapon from his hands. Meanwhile Mavis, in a burst of speed, sent her opponent's weapon flying with a hard-hitting swing.

The beastmen's weapons were designed for one-handed attacks and couldn't stand up to the force of Mile and Mavis's two-handed sword strikes. However, losing to a human in a contest of strength was unthinkable for beastmen—much less against a pair of young, weak-looking little girls.

It was an utter defeat.

Perhaps because there was no way that they could face two sword-wielding opponents empty-handed—no matter how strong they were—or perhaps because they were in such shock from being outclassed by a pair of little human girls, the two who lost their weapons stood stock-still. Mile and Mavis struck them in the guts, and they quickly hit the ground.

The last pair of enemies rushed in after a beat, charging from behind at Reina and Pauline. The mages leapt forward and ran behind Mile and Mavis, only stopping to begin chanting another round of attack spells.

Before them stood Mile and Mavis, swords brandished. Reina and Pauline chanted behind the swordswomen, arming their spells.

Only two remained standing now. Two out of a group of eight.

The beastmen were incredibly rattled, but they couldn't run away and leave their felled allies behind. With dire but determined expressions, they faced the Crimson Vow.

But then...

"Run, now!" Reina commanded.

"Okay!" the three girls called.

All four members of the Crimson Vow ran. It was easy, since they weren't exactly surrounded by enemies anymore.

For a short while, the enemies they left behind were frozen in place, their mouths hanging open dumbly. Then they remembered themselves and quickly moved to help their allies. All the while, they gave thanks to whatever god had smiled down upon them.

They lent a hand to the more injured members and, along with their allies, beat a hasty retreat.

"Just as we planned. Let's go," Reina whispered.

"Roger that!" the other three replied.

The Crimson Vow moved quietly through the underbrush. They were tracking the beastmen.

If they had captured and questioned them, there was no guarantee the beastmen would be truthful in their answers. Besides, dragging along that many prisoners would slow their progress immensely. That said, they couldn't just leave them to run amok in the forest. And they couldn't just kill them.

"Let them go free and follow them." It was a standard maneuver the party kept at their disposal, just in case of situations like this. It was useful, even if it didn't have an especially creative name.

Normally, it would be difficult to track beastpeople, whose hearing and sense of smell far exceeded most humans'. For the Crimson Vow to remain at a safe but trackable distance, where they would not lose sight of their quarry in the forest, would require them to stay within range of the beastmen's sharp senses. However, the men were preoccupied at the moment. The smell of blood and singed fur swirled around them. Several were giddy with pain and proceeded with a far more jarring gait than usual, so they weren't able to pay anywhere near their usual attention to their surroundings.

If they used Mile's detection magic, they would have followed the beastmen from a much safer distance. However, for the sake of the party, Mile wouldn't allow that. Instead, she elected to track the beastmen the old-fashioned way. Thankfully, the circumstances allowed them to do so.

"What...is this?" Reina uttered.

The shock was understandable. What the girls saw as they peeked through the trees was the beastmen assisting their injured fellows into one of five crudely fashioned shacks that now stood before them.

That was fine. The *problem* was the scene unfolding beyond that.

They appeared to be ruins, hewn of quarried rock but half-crumbling. Among them was a great number of beastpeople, working with plows, hoes, and other farming tools.

Mile's initial impression was that of an archaeological dig site, and perhaps that truly was what was going on.

"What do we do?" asked Mavis.

"I mean, what *can* we do?" Pauline replied, concerned. Reina, still shocked, was at a loss for words.

"This is a reconnaissance mission," Mile snapped. "Of course, it's important for us to get this information back to the guild right away. But if there are any clues here that might lead us to the missing hunters, or if there's something here that directly affected them, then there's still a chance that we may make it in time to help them.

"Plus, if the missing people have been captured and we were to show up with a bunch of fighters, then they might run off with them, or take them hostage, or kill them as an example..."

"We'll search the area tonight!"

The moment Mile said the word "hostage," the look in Reina's eyes changed. More than likely, she was recalling her father's final moments.

After they had observed the site for some time, someone came running out of the hut that they had seen the beastmen enter previously. A number of others shortly ran in and out as well, making a huge fuss until eventually everything appeared to be settled.

It didn't seem like they planned to pursue the Crimson Vow. The beastpeople probably figured the girls knew nothing of this place and were just a group of hapless rookie hunters who wandered too deep into the forest. They seemed to have decided the girls were harmless.

They had no clue they were full-fledged hunters or that they had come in pursuit of their fellows. To the beastpeople, they were rookies who had encountered beastmen and fled in terror.

After inflicting harm, of course.

Thankfully, the excavation site was upwind from them, so the beastpeople, even with their sensitive noses, couldn't catch their scent. They had planned it that way, noting the changes in the wind as they tracked the beastmen.

Mile, who had loved a certain book in her previous life, would never overlook such a detail.

Indeed, *that* book. The one that said: "Though you stood downwind, you fools never noticed me!"

"All right, here's the plan."

The Crimson Vow had moved to a place a bit farther downwind from the excavation site, so as not to be discovered, and went over their plan as they ate.

They had plenty of time to cook, but to minimize the risk of discovery, they refused to light a fire. Their meal consisted of hardtack, dried meat, and water.

It was a bit early for dinner, but it wouldn't do to mobilize immediately after eating. They had decided to eat sooner and keep their meal light.

"There are five huts in total. If anyone has been captured, they have to be in one of those," Reina explained. "If we observe the comings and goings for a while, we should spot anything suspicious, but the risk of being noticed is high, and we don't have all that much time. Even if we spot something suspicious, there's no way to confirm it, and if there aren't any captives here in the first place, we'd never be able to tell. So observation is out."

The others nodded. With this many unimpeded beastpeople milling around, the risk of them being spotted was far too great.

"On the other hand, it would be too dangerous to sneak inside the huts. For one, we'd definitely be found out."

"..."

"So, Mile, you're up."

"Huh?" Mile, suddenly thrust into the spotlight, was perplexed.

"Look. We already know you have our best interests in mind. However, people's lives are at stake here. Give it your all, just for this. We need you to use your detection magic at full strength!"

"A-all right."

She had been found out.

Thinking that utilizing her useful magical skills on a daily basis would be bad for her comrades, Mile had been limiting herself to "just a little bit of convenient magic" so they wouldn't be troubled if she wasn't around. Apparently, however, they were aware of this.

Even with that knowledge, though, they never said anything about it.

Mile took a steadying breath. It was time to abandon all restraint.

However, this was a one-time deal. Next job, she would go back to using only so much magic as wouldn't hinder her companions from continuing to take on work, should she disappear. That way, even without her, they would still become amazing hunters.

Of course, her "storage magic" was the exception. Losing that would be incredibly inconvenient, and their earnings would go way down.

She didn't like it, but she would follow the same philosophy as always.

"Now is now, and then is then!"

"Let's go."

"Okay!"

Under cover of darkness, the Crimson Vow moved out, heading for the five small huts.

Their eyes were accustomed to darkness, but there were many among the beastpeople with sharper night vision. Combined with their sense of smell and superb hearing, there was no chance of success without some kind of camouflage.

However, they couldn't afford that luxury. They had to somehow pull this off under their own power. Three of them proceeded nervously.

The fourth, on the other hand...

For now, I'll keep up a barrier that'll keep our scent from circulating through the air. That way, as long as we aren't directly spotted, we should be fine...

Mile wasn't nervous at all.

"The nearest hut is the most suspicious. There are fewer people in that one than the others, and most of them are huddled in one spot. There are only two others in the rest of the space. Also, the reaction I'm getting from them seems more human than beast..."

In truth, she could give them a far more detailed report, but that would be overdoing it. Telling them this much was enough.

Reina immediately understood what this meant: the people in the hut were prisoners and a guard or lookout.

"Let's go..." Reina directed quietly, giving Mile a nod.

The rest nodded in agreement and moved forward, slipping carefully through the trees, avoiding any openings where they would be in clear view.

Mavis suddenly gave a signal. "Get down," she whispered harshly before crouching low to the ground. The rest instinctively dropped as well. Just then, a single beastman passed by their hiding place.

Oh crap, they thought, realizing they had been a bit slow to drop. The beastman appeared not to have noticed. When they looked behind him, they saw tail feathers.

"He's a bird-type," whispered Mavis when it was safe.

"Oh, he's night-blind!" Reina breathed a sigh of relief.

"Why would a bird be the night lookout?" The reasoning was beyond Mile, but she wasn't about to complain.

Maybe someone had complained it was unfair for bird-type beastpeople to avoid taking a turn on the night watch. Normally, such idiocy in the name of "equality" would be insufferable, but right now they were lucky the idiot was on the enemy's side. A great boon, indeed.

After all, the greatest danger is not a fearsome foe but a foolish ally.

In any case, their defense was clearly lacking. The Crimson Vow would find plenty of openings.

It was possible the beastpeople had grown lax, as most people didn't try to navigate the forest at night. And until it had grown dark a short while ago, the open space the beastpeople had occupied had had plenty of lookouts. It was merely chance that the girls had drawn close to where a lookout was stationed. They wouldn't have found this spot before sunset anyway. Not without any signposts or landmarks.

The beastpeople probably assumed the girls who had stumbled into the forest had run home, beelining for the human village on the outskirts of the forest.

The Crimson Vow finally neared the hut, hurrying from tree line to hut wall and clinging to it like shadows.

Like the other four, this hut hadn't been built with any particular forethought. It was a ramshackle construction, as though the beastmen had been in the middle of removing meddlesome trees and suddenly thought, "Hey, you know what? Let's build some huts with these."

There was a bit of a gap between the walls and the roof. Of course, the builders would probably claim that was deliberate. "Oh no, we put that there on purpose! It's for light and ventilation!"

Regardless of why it was there, the gap was an incredibly convenient spot for Mile to peek through. After clambering up the wall and looking through to confirm what was inside, she let off a spell.

"Surround the beastmen with sleeping gas..."

Soon, the two beastmen acting as lookouts fell asleep in their chairs.

What Mile didn't realize was that she was the only one who could ever achieve such an effective result with a spell like that.

No matter what other people said, they would produce no results without conveying the appropriate mental image through their thought pulse. However, Mile, who had a level-5 authorization as far as the nanomachines were concerned, could therefore direct them with verbal instructions. If she just said the right thing, the nanomachines would do her bidding—and with gusto.

Her instructions were a command, from the only level-5 being existing in this world.

Mile merely assumed, *I was thinking of what I wanted while speaking aloud, They just read between the lines.*

The entrance of the hut was on the opposite wall, in view of the other huts and the excavation site. Opening the door would allow light from within to spill out, making their movements more conspicuous.

There was no telling who might be watching, so they couldn't afford such a risk. Instead, they clambered up the wall behind Mile and wedged themselves through the opening.

"Eurgh!!"

They all heard Pauline's groan, but Mile and Reina pointedly ignored it. Undoubtedly, *some* part of her was having difficulty fitting through. *Some* part, indeed.

Though they had all slipped into the hut with relative ease, the two were suddenly stricken by intense displeasure.

"...Who's there?" From the corner of the dark room, a woman's voice called out, questioning. Perhaps to save on oil or candles, the only light within the hut was a low-burning wood fire.

Once their eyes adjusted, they saw a sturdy wooden lattice partitioning one section of the hut into a jail cell. Inside were at least a dozen humans.

"We're thiev... we're hunters who took on a search party job," Mile explained.

"What're little girls like you doin' taking on a dangerous job like this?" asked a middle-aged man who appeared to be a hunter. It wasn't as though they could have known the job would turn into something like this. The others stared warily at the beastmen, though they showed no signs of waking. The four understood the suspicion; status-altering magic and medicinal magic weren't things many people were well versed in.

There were eighteen human captives in total: sixteen men and two women. One of the women looked so young she couldn't possibly be of age yet.

The Crimson Vow had been told there were six hunters, two scholars, and one guild employee on the investigation team. Among the captives before them were a man in his early forties and an airy-seeming, attractive woman of noble birth in her twenties; they were undoubtedly scholars. The pair were probably professor and assistant. Their clothing was sturdy and practical, nothing more than normal cotton garb. No armor at all.

Then there was the lively young teen girl. She wore leather guards that were sturdy and maneuverable but only seemed to do the bare minimum of guarding her most vital points. She was, most likely, the guild master's daughter.

The others had to have been the investigation team's escort, and some hapless hunters who happened to be in the wrong place at the wrong time. There were no women among them; only all-male parties would be foolish enough to take a dangerous job in a strange forest.

"Would you happen to know how much time we have?" Reina asked.

"W-we should be fine," the scholar's assistant answered. "They just changed guards a short while ago, so I don't think anyone will be here before morning."

Naturally, as a professor's assistant, she was quick-witted.

"Just for confirmation, you're the investigation team from the guild, yes?" Mile asked, perhaps a bit tartly.

Even if they denied it, there would be no real way to tell. But waiting for confirmation until they had returned to the capital would have been instant death for the Crimson Vow. It wasn't a risk they could take.

"Yeah, that's right," one of the men replied. "There's nine of us altogether: us six guards, those two scholars, and the little miss there from the guild. Thankfully, all of us are here and safe. The other nine here were two parties who were captured separately at different times, which makes eighteen of us prisoners."

All of the investigation team were here, alive and well. The Crimson Vow beamed internally.

If they were honest, they would admit they thought the team's chances of survival were slim to none, at best. They had hoped that if they were lucky, they would find their bodies. If they weren't, their belongings and the manner of their death, which they would share with the guild. That the entire team was alive? The Crimson Vow were overjoyed. Given that the number of prey animals had decreased due to the changes in the environment, it wouldn't have been unusual if the investigation team had been attacked by some starving predator. Compared to that, being captured by beastpeople was probably preferable. There was a chance of escape or rescue, at least.

In truth, however, there were more than two parties who had gone missing. Perhaps they were also captured by these beastmen and killed or attacked by some fearsome creature.

"Anyway, let's get out of here. We can sit and discuss this once we've escaped," Reina directed.

"Roger that!" The Crimson Vow chirped in immediate reply, but the prisoners looked uneasy.

"Even if we run, we're up against beastmen. They have better night vision and a better sense of smell, not to mention they're strong and agile. I don't think we can outrun them. However, if it's just the four of you, who they don't know about, they probably won't catch up. Go. Report to the guild and our lord! Then they can get a force together, and—"

"We refuse," said Mile.

"Huh?"

Stunned by her sudden refusal, the leader of the investigation team halted mid-sentence.

"If go back without you all, we won't get as high of a reward!" Beside her, Pauline nodded emphatically.

"You idiots. If you get captured, then there'll be no one to tell the guild! The whole thing will start all over again. If we have to go through this whole process again, who knows how long it'll take for us to be rescued!"

Clatter.

As they argued, Mavis's sword flashed. She cleft the sturdy lattice elegantly in twain, freeing the captives from their symbolic prison.

"Whoa!" The captives exclaimed in shock and praise. Mavis shied away, suddenly bashful. She was freeing innocent prisoners from a villain's lair. For Mavis, who longed to be a knight, there was no greater joy.

"Wh..." The guard leader's eyes went wide.

Even wooden, the lattice wasn't so cheaply made that a lady could do away with it with a mere swipe of her sword. Or at least, it *shouldn't* have been. He had long since confirmed it was strong enough to prevent escape.

Though it was unclear whether she read his thoughts, Mavis, having noticed the leader's gaze, muttered with a self-deprecating smirk, "I may as well let you know now, but I'm the weakest of the bunch."

"No," Pauline interjected as she cut through the prisoners' fetters with a Water Cutter, "I'm the weakest."

The leader stared in slack-jawed awe. Just as Mile taught her, Pauline had increased the hydraulic pressure of the water by narrowing the surface area and mixing in grains of sand to create a cutting edge of startling strength and sharpness.

"We don't have time to chitchat! You'll have plenty of time to argue once we get out of here. Now, let's get going!" said Reina.

The hunters nodded, standing one by one after rubbing life back into their freed legs. The leader, with no other choice, stood as well.

"If we don't put out the fire, the light will spill out when we open the door. Use your water magic to—"

Mile interrupted the man again. "Oh, we aren't going out from the front. But we probably should put it out, yes."

Following the leader's advice, Mile extinguished the flame with a wave of her hand. Instantaneously. Without water.

Whish!

"Wh...?"

Mile's arm moved faster than the eye could see, drawing her blade, swinging it, and with the same swift movement, placing it back into its sheath. Then she firmly gripped the wall and pulled.

Suddenly, a hole, wide enough for a crouching adult to pass through, opened up.

"..."

"Now, quickly!"

Mavis hurried along the hunters, who were standing still for some reason. They sputtered wordlessly but silently slipped out through the hole one by one.

Mile went at the head. She had the sharpest night vision, and with her detection magic, she would be the first to know if any monsters drew near. Plus, she could cut a path through the brush for the people following her. Just behind her was Reina, ready to back her with magical attacks.

Mavis took up the rear, prepared to ward off attacks from behind. Pauline kept to the middle, prepped to handle any flanking attacks. She would also be able to jump to the front or the back at a moment's notice.

Naturally, the hunters had had their weapons taken away on capture, leaving them empty-handed and unable to fight. There were four mages among the freed captives, including both women, but of the four, only one man and one woman could use attack spells. It fell on the Crimson Vow to defend the group.

As they moved from the open area into the woods, Mile had a sudden idea. She attached a piece of wood painted with a "magical luminescent material" to each person's back. As they moved with their eyes to the ground, every so often they could look up and not lose sight of the person ahead of them. Naturally, she instructed them to remove the markers at the first sign of an enemy.

Using a regular reflective material in the dark would be fruitless, so this was either a "material with stored luminescence," or "something with luminous material mixed in." However, Mile had passed the duty of making it entirely over to the nanomachines, so she had no idea which it was. So long as it didn't contain radium and subject them all to radiation, as some materials like that did, it was fine.

Once they were a fair distance away from the beastpeople's camp, the group took a break. They were all exhausted. Dashing through the night taxed their physical and emotional strength, not to mention the general exhaustion of hiking through rough terrain. If anyone was injured or collapsed, it would be a huge problem, least of all because their speed would decrease by a great deal.

The beastpeople had yet to notice their escape.

As everyone rested, Mile selected a suitable tree and lopped off a nice-looking branch. And then another and another. When she had collected a good number of them, she whittled them all down at tremendous speed. Naturally, she did so where no one could see her. Then, her work done almost as soon as it had started, she returned to the others, items in hand.

"Everyone, please choose one of these for yourself!"

"Wh..."

The hunters eyes went wide as saucers as the bundle clattered to the group, displaying an array of wooden swords and spears.

"Wh-where did you...?"

"Oh, I just made these."

"..."

After several moments of silence, the hunters quietly began to select their arms. Naturally, as hunters who had purposely taken on a dangerous job, they were quite adaptable.

Though made of wood, the swords and spears wouldn't

shatter or be cleft in a few strikes, even if they clashed with iron. Mile had chosen a firm and sturdy tree. Still, they weren't invulnerable, especially if they came up against someone particularly skilled or with a very good sword.

They had other uses as well, doubling as a staff or walking cane. They would brush branches and tall reedy grass away and ward off animals or monsters. Besides, having so many unarmed hunters would be troublesome. Even if they were all wood, the swords and spears would put them all at ease.

The hunters' expressions were already far more confident than they had been just a short while ago.

Mm-hmm, all according to... plan.

Shing!

A single piercing gaze shot towards Mile.

It was from a girl in her teens. The guild master's daughter. Why was she looking at her like that?

Did she think it looked bad for a guild employee to be rescued by a band of girls the same age or even younger than her? Did she think it would sully her father's reputation as the guild master?

It would probably be best to try and curry her favor.

Thinking this, Mile began to speak.

"Um, we were asked by your father to look out for you..."

"Whaaaaaaaaaaaaaaaaaaaat?!?!" the girl suddenly shouted.

"Shhhhhhhhh!!!"

Everyone turned as one to shush her. Even if they had gotten a fair distance away, it was still dangerous to make loud noises.

"S-sorry about that..." the girl sincerely apologized. "A-anyway, you're saying that you all met my f-father? Wh-where? When?!"

The girl latched onto Mile's words, her cheeks red and her eyes damp.

"Huh? I mean it's not like we just ran into him somewhere. When we were at the capital guild branch, he asked us, 'Look out for my daughter...'"

"Huh?"

"Huh?"

"Huh?"

"Um..." a voice muttered from behind them.

Mile turned to see the professor's pupil—the airy, attractive assistant.

"If you're looking for the guild master's daughter," she said, "That's... me."

"Huh?!" the Crimson Vow gasped.

"No way! There's no way a rough old dude like him could have a daughter like you!" Reina, as always, was incredibly blunt.

The young woman sighed. "I hear that a lot..." She hung her head as though suddenly overcome with exasperation.

"Hm? Then *you* must be the scholar's assistant."

"I'm not!"

"Huh?"

Then who was this little girl? As the Crimson Vow nearly tore their hair out over this conundrum, another voice came from behind.

"I'm the assistant," the man in his forties said.

"*You* are? Uhh, th-then, that means the professor is..."

"That's right! I am Doctor Clairia, or as you all put it, the 'professor,'" the little girl quipped with a grandiose manner. She puffed out her nonexistent chest.

"A dwarf?"

"I'm an elf!"

"*Shhhhhhh!*"

"S-so sorry..."

CHAPTER 29 |

Demonic Deeds

FINALLY, THE ESCAPE PARTY was on the move again.

They had hoped to discuss a number of things on their break, but between everyone catching their breath, Mile's errand, everyone choosing weapons, and settling the commotion that followed, there was no time left to consider anything further.

They couldn't waste any more time and were likely to take more breaks anyway. They decided to talk more on their next rest. Carrying on heavy conversation while walking single file through the forest at night was beyond the abilities of most people anyway.

After they had walked for some time, Mile picked up a strange reaction on her radar.

Brown?

If it was someone peaceful, they were blue; if they were hostile, red. Those who were neither were yellow. Anyone between those categories showed up in varying shades of the colors. But a little way ahead of them, there was *brown*. Was it brown, or was it ochre? Either way, they were incredibly close.

The brownish marking was completely still, off to the side of their path. It was very near. And soon enough, she saw it.

The droppings of an enormous animal.

Apparently, the marking had been a warning against stepping, or rather, plunging into the pile. Pointless, but blessedly convenient.

Oh, that's right!

As something flashed into Mile's mind, she turned and indicated to the group behind her. "Watch out! There's a big pile of poop over here. Anyway, let's take another short rest up ahead."

The others behind her passed through, cautious of the droppings, then walked ahead until they found an appropriate place for a break.

Mile stepped away, back to where she had been standing before.

"Now, if I make a thin container out of earth, and strengthen the outside of it with a magical coating, and put some of this dung inside..."

Naturally, she wouldn't fill the vessel with dung by hand but with magic.

Then Mile did something particularly suspicious.

"The off-putting stench of a fart comes from proteins...gases like ammonia, hydrogen sulfide, indole, skatole, volatile amines, and so forth. Or so I remember reading..."

She took some things from her inventory and placed them into the vessel, transforming and mixing them together with magic. Finally, she plopped a peculiar pebble down into it.

This pebble was Mile's handcrafted Magic Pebble of Extended Radiation. "For twenty-four hours, or until the container is broken, continue to generate heat," she instructed, which the nanomachines clinging to the pebble had no choice but to obey. However, the moment that the pebble was dropped into the vessel, they understood their fate.

Gaaaaaaaaaaaaaaaaaaaaaaaaaaaaahh!!!

From somewhere, tiny screams could be heard.

After putting a lid on the vessel, she used magic to coat the outside, then carefully placed it in the crook of a tree. Then she took a white handkerchief from her pocket and tied it to the branch.

It was a roundabout sign but clearly visibly. Plus, it had Mile's scent, so there was little chance the beastmen would miss it.

"Sorry to keep you waiting," she called as she moved. "Now let's get going again!"

Mile returned to the others, looking as though nothing at all were wrong. She took her place once again at the head of the line.

Around sunrise the next morning, a guard headed toward the prisoners' hut to relieve the night watch. When he opened the door, however, he was greeted with an alarming sight.

The wooden lattice had been cut to pieces by something sharp edged. The fetters were shattered. The watchmen sat slumped in their chairs, unconscious. Worst of all, a large, semicircular hole had been ripped in the wall opposite the entrance.

"Th-they've escaped!!!"

The guard's voice rang out across the camp.

"Damn it, this is why I said build a sounder structure!"

A recovery team was hastily thrown together. The man in charge grumbled as he ran.

All told, the fact he hadn't grumbled "We should've just killed them" was probably proof these beastmen weren't bad people. However, good or bad, a soldier on the battlefield never hesitated to kill his opponent. That was the only thing to do. "Good" and "evil" were relative concepts, a judgment based only on the number of living creatures in the world.

Well, no. No, perhaps there were even more things than that. Intelligent machines and other inscrutable creatures beyond the realm of the living...

There were twenty beastmen in the quickly assembled team.

Upon investigation, they realized the prisoners hadn't retrieved their weapons, which meant the beastmen couldn't fail—certainly not in a battle against empty-handed humans running through the forest. Ten of them alone could have easily apprehend the escapees, but there was a possibility others had come to their rescue. They had no way of knowing exactly how many rescuers there were or how many people in the forest. So for safety's sake, they had formed a band of twenty.

Someone questioned whether this might be the work of the female hunters they had encountered at midday. But that was unfathomable. A group of young girls who had been scared off by them earlier, attempting such a rescue? Unthinkable. Admittedly, it *was* suspicious that the interception team had come back so injured and that they had scared the girls off but not captured them. But that wasn't an issue, not in the grand scheme of things.

It wasn't as though they had led the girls to the excavation site, or even let them know about its existence, after all. The girls met beastmen in the woods and ran home scared. That was all that happened. So long as the girls hadn't been injured, it was fine. Besides, it was best not to take more unnecessary prisoners.

Or so the leader of the recovery team thought.

If no real problems arose, then the humans wouldn't bother the beastmen. Their relationship wasn't particularly good in the first place, but they managed to maintain something like peace. And surely, both sides would want to avoid any circumstances that could lead to war.

Should things between the beastmen and the humans turn sour, whoever was responsible would bear the brunt of the blame from their fellow humans. Acting rashly was the furthest thing from anyone's mind.

And so long as no one found out what they were doing...

They *had* to find those escaped humans.

If the humans learned about the captives they had taken, it was unlikely they would do anything right away. So the beastmen would have some time, but they needed to prepare to retreat at a moment's notice. They could probably manage that in another ten days.

The humans, whose night vision was poor, couldn't have gotten far in the middle of the night. Fatigue and diminished mental states would have slowed them down. Coupled with the brashness of the escape and their need for distance, by now they were sure to be exhausted and immobilized by injury. It was a truly foolish gambit.

The leader considered these things as he followed the forward scout. A young thing, he had been selected based on his sharp sense of smell and vision, as well as his natural powers of deduction. The scout came to a sudden halt. The leader stopped just in time, only narrowly avoiding crashing into him. The rest of the recovery team stopped as well, gathering around to see what was going on.

"What's wrong?"

"Over there..."

They followed his pointing to a tree, where a white cloth was tied to a branch like a sign post; in the crook sat a pot-like container.

"What is that?"

"Who knows?"

There was no use in standing around pondering. Time was precious today. The longer they stood gaping at a tree, the further their targets got away.

That said, they couldn't leave such a suspicious object alone.

"Did they think it would be too much of a hassle to transport that thing with them and left it there with a marker to retrieve later? They must have figured we wouldn't be able to follow their tracks that well and wouldn't come across it. Or else..."

It was a trap.

They halted in their tracks.

It could be a trap. But it might not be. There was no reason the humans would bother carrying such a heavy-looking, awkward thing. Come to think of it, why on earth would people who were part of an investigation team or a missing persons search party, who knew nothing about the beastpeople, carry such a thing?

"Do you think it's something they found near the dig site? Something they wanted to take back with them? Wait. Is it, is it the thing that we're..."

By now, they had all reached the same conclusion.

"We need to know! Be careful, take it down gently!"

At the leader's direction, several young beastmen gathered around the tree. The moment they laid their fingers on the vessel, nestled in a crook about five feet off the ground, the vessel's magical coating disintegrated.

Bang!

With an explosive sound, the vessel shattered. Its contents flew everywhere.

The vessel itself was made of nothing more than earth, and so it was very thin; the coating on the outside had been the only thing keeping it from self-destructing. Without it, the vessel would have long since shattered under the weight of its own contents before the heat and internal pressure could even rise to the appropriate levels.

The vessel itself posed little threat to the beastmen.

Its contents, however...

Flop.

Plop plop.

Several of the twenty silently fainted at once.

Some of them stood wide-eyed, foaming at the mouth. Others wet themselves in a fit of incontinence. And those who had the misfortune of getting it into their mouths...

Hurk!

Gaaaaaaah!

Many lost the contents of their stomachs. Others, try as they may to cover their noses and mouths, were struck with a severe bout of the runs as their minds went hazy.

"R-retreat! Grab the fallen and get out of here!" the leader directed, once he had vomited until there was nothing left but bile. "If we leave them here, they'll die!!!" The beastmen who had wanted to run immediately mustered their self-restraint, rushing to their fallen allies' sides and dragging them away.

The men who had been doused in the mysterious goop smelled horrendous. This was far beyond what the beastmen, with their sharp noses, could bear. They vomited as they carried their fallen comrades, their faces moist with snot and tears, doing their best to stay conscious. It wasn't long before those carrying the fallen couldn't bear it. They soon collapsed themselves.

"Take off your clothes! Breathe through your mouths and stay awake!"

The sooner they got their goop-soaked clothes off, the better. After that, they just had to get away as quickly as possible.

Tracking and capturing the humans as soon as possible? That was out of the question now. It would be several days before their sense of smell recovered, not to mention the exhaustion that came with vomiting and carrying their allies..

Fighting people? While they were so exhausted from puking that they could barely even stand straight?

"We need water, immediately," the leader said. "We can get back to the dig site after that." He pointed them in a new direction.

If they returned like this, everyone at the campsite would be ruined as well. *That* was how horrific the smell was.

The leader, face twisted in anguish, muttered. "This is the work of a demon..."

At that very moment, countless tiny beings—invisible to the human eye—who had been thrown from the exploded vessel, flew at top speed to the nearest water source, wailing all the way.

The recovery party returned to camp after midday. The remaining beastpeople refused to let them approach the huts, so after putting a fair bit of distance between them, the recovery party shouted their report. After hearing this, the commander of the beastmen assembled a new team.

If their enemy was going to employ such dirty tactics, they weren't going to fight them fair and square. The second group, an interception team, was a group of twelve, selected for their agility.

At least, that was what the commander would say if anyone were to question him. In truth, while they assumed the strength of the escapees to be low, they just couldn't afford to spare any more fighters. Certainly not if they all came back like this.

Several of them had returned the day before with a startling number of injuries. Now, twenty more men were out of commission. Excluding those with more specialized skill sets and jobs—such as lookouts, scouts, and camp guards when things were dire—most of the residents were laborers or support workers. Their fighting forces came from a very shallow, very limited, pool, indeed.

It was unthinkable to send out laborers, women, or youths who had been brought along for miscellaneous tasks. No matter how weak their enemies might be, they couldn't take such a risk.

Plus, the proud beastmen would never send all the able-bodied young workers away and leave the older, the injured, and the women to fend for themselves. To do such a thing would be a failing for their race, and *that* wasn't something they could even consider.

It would probably take the half-blind, fragile humans—who were also dragging along non-hunters—two days to make it through the forest. Half a day had already passed since they fled.

However, if a small group of beastmen went after them at full clip, they could overtake the humans without much difficulty. The humans would have to sleep eventually; otherwise, they wouldn't have the strength to go on. The beastmen had gotten a full night's rest, and could easily go a day and a half without sleeping. A few short breaks were enough for them.

With all this in mind, the commander sent out the new team—after being pressed again and again by the first team about the "place they must absolutely avoid."

"It's coming up soon. Take caution... Gwah!"

Just as the leader of the second recovery team issued a warning, they neared *it*.

"Evade! Take a wide detour!"

A faint, distant whiff of the stench, carried on the wind, was enough to make him gag.

Edging away from the smell and the feeling of nausea, the leader redirected the group, giving the location a huge berth. It was some time before he picked up the escaped humans' smell again.

Though the first couple of breaks were taken up by everyone catching their breath—and Mile enacting her plan—during the breaks afterward, the Crimson Vow was finally able to gather some information from the former captives.

It was difficult to move well at night, so they took most of their breaks then. If they let fatigue undermine them—if any of them ended up injured—their progress would be even slower. So, when they stopped for a longer rest, Mile brought out easily-digestible food and water from her inventory to pass around. They enjoyed a light meal and conference.

Tiffy, the guild employee, did most of the explaining. According to her, the local lord had offered a pittance to have a team investigate the strange happenings in the forest. The team was put together, comprised of Dr. Clairia, a specialist in forest ecology; her assistant, who had been invited from the royal capital; a handful of hunters as escorts; and Tiffy, the guild employee.

Though the lord was funding it, gathering the team had been a guild undertaking. One that had been thrust on it. Tiffy insinuated it hadn't been so much leaving things to the guild's discretion as shoving the responsibility onto it, in the event things went awry. However, this didn't matter to the Crimson Vow.

Additionally, it was out of concern for Dr. Clairia, the only woman in the group, that Tiffy had volunteered to accompany them. Of course, the Crimson Vow had already heard as much from the guild master.

"And then, while we were in the middle of our investigation, we were surrounded by a large group of beastmen and captured."

"..." The four girls silently listened to Tiffy's story.

"And... that's all."

"Huh?!"

"That's it. That's how things ended up this way."

"Too short! That explanation was way too short!!!" the four cut in, well trained now by Mile.

"Wh-what is it with these beastmen?! What are they doing out there?!" Reina prodded further.

Indeed, this wasn't something that could go unaddressed.

"Ah, it seems they're searching for something, although we never managed to ask them directly. We just overheard bits and pieces of their conversations."

What good is thaaat?!?! As a crestfallen air fell over the Crimson Vow, a voice spoke up from behind them.

"They appear to be excavating something," Dr. Clairia explained. "I don't believe they're digging for ore, but perhaps an artifact in some ruins... However, I don't think they've discovered anything, and they don't seem confident that the item they're after is there at all. They believe it *might* be there. Their target is apparently an incredibly classified item, so much so they aren't entirely sure what it is. They were likely hired by someone else, who entrusted them to work the site."

Mile nodded in agreement. "This is all so secretive," she noted, "but it seems like you found out a lot about it, Doctor."

The scholar looked triumphant.

"I used a special technique handed down amongst elves for dealing with humans and beastmen."

"Wow, that's awesome! What kind of technique is it?"

Perhaps because she couldn't bear to be cruel to Mile, who looked at her with sparkling, expectant eyes, or perhaps because she wanted to brag a bit, Clairia gloated as she explained.

"Here's what you do. First you put your hands together and place them under your chin. Then you wet your eyes and say the following: 'I'm boooored. Will you tell me a story, Mister?'"

Whaaaaaaaaaaaaaaat?!

Because Clairia was an elf, she appeared no more than fifteen or sixteen. In truth, she was much, *much...*

They're terrifying! Elves are terrifying!

All the men in the group suddenly trembled in fear.

Elves in this world didn't have long ears that grew out to the sides like the ones in Japanese manga. The ones with the pointiest ears might look like someone from the fabled planet Vulcan at best, and there were even those whose ears were barely any more pointed than a human's. And so, there were plenty of cases where, if their ears were covered with their hair, you couldn't even tell.

There was no doubt the beastmen would have thought Clairia to be another rookie hunter or something. Just like Mile and the others had.

Unlike the commander of the beastmen, Mile estimated it would take their party about a day and a half to reach the village on the outskirts of the forest. Such calculations were often her strong point, so long as no human factors got involved.

The commander couldn't help making such a mistake in his estimation. There was no way he could know the escapees were led by someone with sharper night vision than a beastperson, or that they had more than enough food and water without having to carry it themselves, or that they used luminescent markings to follow each other and never get lost.

Plus, when Mile confirmed things with Dr. Clairia, her assistant, and Tiffy, the guild employee—all assumed to be the cause of any delays—the following transpired:

"Are you underestimating elves? Who live in the woods?" Dr. Clairia demanded.

"Do you know what it means to assist a professor who's *always* pursuing field work?" her assistant asked.

"You know I'm an employee of the guild, right? And moreover, just who my father is? Oh, and that I'm a C-rank hunter?" Tiffy challenged.

Naturally, the 'what' referred to his position as the guild master...

After some thinking, Mile deemed it difficult for the escapees, who, on top of being exhausted from their imprisonment, had made their escape in the dead of night, to make it all the way to the village on only a series of short rests that were little more than a breather. Even if they could stay awake the whole time, their fatigue would only grow. Their attention wavering, people would begin stumbling and probably eventually sprain something. If that happened, their rate of travel would decrease immensely.

They had no choice but to stop for several hours, have a bit of food, and get some real rest.

Should the beastmen find the trap and lose their sense of smell, and thus their tracking skills, they would have to return to the excavation to form a new team. They would lose about half a day. Even if the trap didn't work *that* well, it would still take them several hours to fully recover their sense of smell.

In truth, the trap turned out to be far more effective than Mile imagined, but she had no way of knowing this.

In any case, for now, the escapees and the Crimson Vow had to put as much distance behind them as they could before their fatigue reached its peak. They had no other choice.

After walking through the night, and through to sunset the next day without the beastmen catching up, they finally stopped for a proper meal and a good, long sleep. The following day, they intended to leave as soon as it was light enough to do so. They would ignore the village on the outskirts of the forest and head for the regional capital, where they should arrive by dusk.

The way things stood, the village wasn't safe for them, not while so many beastmen roamed the forest. Rather than put the villagers in danger, it was much better for them to go straight to the capital.

The former captives ate their fill of their first hot meal in some time and then laid down to sleep. All except for Mile, who had been casually pulling food, folded tents, blankets, and such from her inventory. And the loli-grandma—that is, *Clairia*—who stared at the half-eaten food left on the dishes and noticed how *fresh* all the vegetables and meat had been…

CHAPTER 30

A Fearsome Fight! The Sunrise Battle

I T WAS BEFORE SUNRISE, when the skies were still murky.

Mile had already woken everyone and prepared a hasty breakfast of hardtack, dried meat, and rehydrated soup. She now made preparations for their departure.

"They're here," she said quietly. "Twelve people behind us. It doesn't seem they've actually spotted us yet."

"How do you know?" asked the leader of the hunters.

"Are you going to violate the Hunters' Code and ask about my skills?" Mile chided.

"Erk... S-sorry," he apologized.

Unlike with Dragonbreath, whom they had previously been partnered, she had to be strict about these matters.

Well, with a party like the escorts of the investigation team, a bunch of serious sticklers who would take on such a tough and non-lucrative job like this, she had to be this way.

"We'll have to defend ourselves. We'll leave the direction of the investigation team and the other parties up to you. Please make sure no one is killed or carried off. Minor injuries are okay within reason," said Reina.

"N-now just hang on! What the heck are you planning to do?! Besides, I should be the one to direct everyone," the leader complained.

"And just what do you plan to do, when you don't even have proper weapons?" Reina asked. "We accepted a job to locate and rescue the investigation team. Therefore, in order to save you all, we need to defeat these enemies. The job you took is to protect the scholars, isn't it? So you need to stay behind and protect them."

"Wh..." The leader, being treated so lightly by Reina, who was a child in his eyes, was dumbfounded.

She was right, however. There was no way wooden swords and spears would be reliable against enemies outfitted with metal weaponry. Fighting monsters would be one thing, but in a battle against beastmen, they would have to fend off attacks with all their might. A proper clash would see their wooden arms shattered into little pieces.

"Th-the two frontline fighters could lend us your swords..."

"You really think we'd hand over our beloved swords to strangers just before a big battle?!" Mavis raged.

"Guess you're right..." the leader agreed, his shoulders slumped. Apparently, even he was aware of how ridiculous he sounded.

"Don't need to worry so much. Just yesterday, we fought off eight of those beastmen on our own," Pauline added.

"Wh-what?"

The leader's eyes widened in disbelief. He had assumed the girls had managed to make it to the huts by slipping through the beastpeople's surveillance network, managing not to run into any enemies along the way.

"We haven't any time," said Mile, interrupting. "If they spot us, they'll try to surround us. We can assume they'll want to capture every one of us, to keep any information from getting out. It's too late for us to run now, so we'll stand here and face them."

"Understood."

There was no more time to stand around and talk. The leader gave a reluctant nod.

"There they are! It looks like they're already awake and on the move."

"I see..."

The humans had been moving more quickly than expected, so despite hurrying along, the beastmen had yet to catch up with the escapees. However, the interception team still overtook them before they could leave the forest.

For a short while, there had been signs they were drawing near. They had assumed, should all go well, that they would strike while their enemies were still sleeping. But the humans had awoken before dawn and were already making preparations.

Granted, attacking their enemies in their sleep wasn't a tactic the proud beastmen preferred. However, this wasn't an ordinary fight. They were recapturing escaped prisoners and would use any means necessary to secure them. For the sake of their allies back at the dig site, they couldn't allow the humans to get away.

As their opponents were unarmed, this wasn't much of a 'battle,' anyway, but more of a 'capture.' Attacking them by surprise this time would help ensure no one on the other side was injured, and therefore it need not be a blow to the beastmen's pride.

That was how the second retrieval team had been made to understand it. Their leader, to assuage their anxieties, had explained it simply: "We beastmen are a proud race. If we ever sully the names of our people, our families, or ourselves—if we bring shame upon them—this sin can be cleansed only by death. Wouldn't a sneak attack be disgraceful for proud soldiers such as we?"

However, as they weren't able use the sneak attack after all, such concerns of honor ended up moot. They shook their heads at themselves.

Even so, the situation wasn't problematic yet. They faced eighteen unarmed humans, with non-combatants in their midst. Even if several rescuers arrived, there was no way normal humans could stand up to beastmen in serious combat.

Believing this, the leader—relieved they had caught up— didn't doubt their success.

"Okay boys, surround 'em. Once we have, we'll close the perimeter. When they spot us, we'll show ourselves as one and demand their surrender."

Even if the humans intended to fight, seeing they had been discovered and surrounded should be enough to make them surrender. They should know that no harm would come to them even if they were captured and that they would be released as soon as the beastmen were finished with their business. They had told the humans so over and over. Given the kind treatment they had been shown until now, hopefully they believed it.

Therefore, he couldn't imagine them resisting to the death, not without any arms.

And indeed, his assumption was correct.

At least, until the Crimson Vow arrived...

"There they are!"

Mavis's shout put everyone on edge. Tension flooded the hands that gripped various weapons.

The Crimson Vow had expected pursuers, but not only twelve of them. They thought there would be at least a few more. However, they couldn't have predicted the eight men from their first encounter would withhold information about the girls' strength to save face. And Mile was the only one who knew about the trap. This was a surprise, but it wasn't exactly going to be a *problem* for them.

Once they realized the escapees had spotted them, the beastmen jumped into view. Encircling the group, they began to close in. Before the escapees, who stood with their backs to a large tree, were four young girls the men didn't recognize. They were positioned as if to protect the others.

Are they the ones who came to rescue the prisoners? Four little girls... Are they the all-female party the interception team spoke of the other day? The ones they chased away?! Those idiots! They were followed!

The leader now understood how the prisoners had escaped. However, now wasn't the time to stop and ponder this.

"As you can see, you are surrounded. Surrender. Don't do anything stupid. The only ones with proper weapons are those two young ladies in front, so there's nothing you can do. We don't intend to hurt you, do you understand?"

The leader was a bit rattled to see the escapees all outfitted with what were most assuredly 'weapons,' wooden though they may be, but he didn't allow it to show on his face. That was the most basic tenet of negotiation.

However, the Crimson Vow stood firm.

"Why should we listen to a bunch of bandits and turn ourselves over? You think we're stupid?"

"What?! We aren't bandits!" the leader of the beastmen shouted indignantly. Reina was undeterred.

"You attacked this group in the middle of the woods, took their weapons and belongings, and locked them up! If that's not the work of bandits, then what is? Are you criminals, or is banditry normal for beastpeople? If that's the case, we need to let the capital know so word can get around. As long as people are properly aware of your customs, then such misunderstandings can be avoided in the future. Would you mind telling us your names? We need to share the names of the brave beastmen who provided this valuable information, after all!"

"Wh-wh-wha..." Reina's over-the-top proposal left the leader speechless.

If those kinds of rumors got around, the beastmen's reputation would be ground into the dirt. And with their names attached, they and all of their kin would be barred from living in their villages again.

However, what the girl said wasn't entirely wrong. At this rate, the good name of beastpeople was going to be sullied, all because of them.

The only thing they could do now was capture everyone present and take them back to camp. Then they would return the humans' belongings upon releasing them, telling them the truth of the situation when they did so as to clear up any misunderstandings.

"...Guess we got no choice. We didn't wanna get rough with you, but if that's how you're gonna be, then we'll have to show you our true strength!"

"Oh, your true strength?" Reina was grinning.

Seeing this, the leader commanded in a sharp voice, "Attack!"

The beastmen harbored no ill intent toward the humans, and in fact, upon first capturing the investigation team and the hunters, they had taken care not to harm anyone.

Fighting against someone you knew had no intent to kill or injure gave you an advantageous position in battle. The Crimson

Vow had discussed just such advantage before the beastmen arrived. Therefore, the four girls decided to hold back a bit, as well.

Save for Pauline.

"Ultra Hot Shower!!!"

Fwshhhhhh!

A garishly crimson liquid rained down on the three beastmen facing Pauline.

"Gaaaaaaaaaaaaaaah!!!"

For the beastmen, with their sharp senses of smell and sight, this was incredibly, incredibly, *incredibly* painful...

Two of them were rolling around on the ground. And the third? He fainted immediately.

A fourth of the recovery team was out already.

$12 \div 4 = 3$

Pauline's work was done. However, she already had her next spell ready. Just in case.

"True Godspeed Blade, 1.4 Speed!!!"

Beastpeople were faster and stronger than humans. If Mavis didn't go full force from the very start, fighting against even one of them would be a trial; challenging three could mean instant death.

However, beastpeople weren't *too* much faster than humans. Up against a human with sufficient training, the difference was small, at best.

Of course in the heat of battle, that small difference could make or break you.

However, Mavis was equipped with the True Godspeed Blade.

She might not be able to cross swords with three beastmen using the normal Godspeed Blade she acquired through her own hard work, but with the True Godspeed Blade—obtained through body-strengthening magic—she became a self-styled 1.4 times faster. (It was, actually, about 1.3 times her usual speed, and perhaps only somewhere between 1.15 and 1.2 times faster than the average A-rank hunter.) Mavis already had a lot of potential, but with this she became a formidable force.

However, this didn't mean Mavis could win against an A-rank hunter. Factor in differences in skill, experience, tactics, and stamina, and such a thing was out of the question. But fighting beastmen, who preferred to rely on strength and loathed technique, she had a good chance of an even match.

And of course, there was a difference in their weapons.

The beastmen carried machetes, hatchets, and other things not designed for battle. Compared to Mavis's short sword, which had far better reach and speed for swing, they were at a distinct disadvantage.

Above all else, Mavis was a swordswoman who practiced on a regular basis, and she fought with civilians at her back. For someone who aimed to be a knight, no one—no matter how skilled or how physically fit—could beat her spirit.

With a roar, she dashed forward.

Introducing a great deal of force stiffened the sinews and forced one's speed to drop. She dropped a bit of her strength, to move at 100 percent speed!

She was up against machetes and hatchets, but Mavis, who knew which way the blades were going to move, had absolute faith in her beloved, unbreakable sword.

She moved a split-second faster than her enemy could read and prepare for. Their blades clashed at an odd angle, such that if her timing had been off, her weapon could have been thrown back or struck from her hands. Mavis turned the sword ninety degrees and struck it hard into her enemy's guts.

Being that it was a double-edged blade, there was no point in striking with the back of the sword. They would have died.

"Gwah!"

"Urk!"

Two of the beastmen fell to the ground. The third stood and stared, his eyes wide in disbelief.

Reina, on the other hand, had begun the fight at a disadvantage.

Because she had been speaking to the leader until the fight began, she hadn't had a chance to prepare a spell ahead of time.

By all measures, fighting in melee range against enemies who were quick and skilled in close-range combat, without any prior preparation, was a situation most mages hoped to avoid at all costs.

And yet...

"Guh!" The beastman who tried to rush her met the pointed end of a staff to the gut. He was almost immediately immobilized.

"Wh..."

Of the three beastmen facing her, two now remained, the undeserved grins upon their faces twitching.

One of them alone should have been enough to take an unprepared mage; a small human girl, no less. Or so the two had assumed, leading them to hang back casually. Now, they tried to quickly summon their strength, but it was already too late. While Reina swung her staff at the first beastman, she had been chanting a spell. Now that relatively short incantation was complete.

"Hot Inferno!"

A mild whirlwind whipped up, swirling gently around the beastmen. The air turned a little reddish.

"Gyeeeeeeee!!!"

The three beastmen, including the one who had already fallen, rolled on the ground, clawing at their throats. Tears streamed from their tightly shut eyes, and snot dripped from their noses.

At least for now, Reina remembered to use non-lethal magic. As she said to Mile and Pauline:

"As long as it's non-lethal, it doesn't matter if allies or other bystanders catch friendly fire. It uses up less magical energy than any large-scale flame spell."

Upon hearing this from her, Mavis had sputtered in disbelief, but Pauline nodded in agreement. *Amazing, non-lethal magic!* Mile had initially thought. *Something someone cool like 'Stern the Destroyer' would use...*

But not Starlight Breaker, absolutely not! If she used that, someone would definitely die!

She had elected *not* to teach that to Reina. Even Mile had some common sense, now and then.

The beastmen's leader was part of the trio facing Mile.

Normally, the leader, the strongest of their group, would go up against Mavis, seemingly the strongest of the Crimson Vow and a swordswoman. That was what Mile assumed, but perhaps thanks to his instincts, the leader realized Mile was the strongest of the four. Unfortunately for him, he didn't know just *how* strong she was.

Just as Mile moved to deflect his knife, a ball of flame flew toward her from behind him.

"A-an attack spell?"

Magic was a weak point for most beastpeople, whose power lacked in comparison to humans. However, that was only true for the *majority* of beastpeople. There were many who couldn't use magic at all, and many whose limited magic was far weaker than the average human's. However, among them also existed those whose magic was as strong, or stronger, than a human's. That number just happened to be much lower.

That said, there were far fewer beastpeople than humans to begin with, so the observation that "there are no beastpeople good with magic" was an understandable misrepresentation.

Naturally, those few beastpeople who *did* have strong magic were sent to the front lines.

The leader and the mage. The two strongest members of their team were both facing off against Mile. They must have had a very high opinion of her.

Mile, who had assumed beastmen couldn't use magic, was thrown off by the sudden magical attack... *not*. As she swung her sword two-handed, she pulled her left hand away. She repelled the leader's knife with her right hand alone and redirected the flame orb with the back of her left.

The flame orb shot straight into the gut of the third beastman, who had the misfortune of standing behind the leader.

"Wh..." The leader and the mage froze, watching as the orb blew their companion back.

Because it had been fired without intent to harm, it didn't explode on impact. Instead it scattered, dissipating when it reached its intended target, its surface temperature low to begin with. What had sent the beastman flying back was half-shock, half-him trying to renegotiate his own stance. He hadn't really taken much damage at all.

However, the mage was terribly shaken and unable to prepare his next spell. The leader stood stock-still as well, his blade still crossed against Mile's.

"Hup!"

Mile pushed her sword forward, flinging the leader's knife away. She struck him in the side with her sword.

The mage, who had returned to his senses, began to incant a spell but discarded it halfway. He realized what was going on around him. Mavis had felled her third opponent, leaving him and the relatively undamaged youth who had been thrown back by the repelled flame orb the only remaining combat-capable fighters.

The mage understood: Their chances of victory were now zero. If the two of them fell as well, it would spell doom for their companions.

It wasn't as though the humans, who probably wished to leave, had gravely injured them. Yet, even if they just left them here, not killing them out of fear of war between humans and beastpeople, there was no telling how many days it would take them to get back to the worksite. Nor how many it would take before the others grew worried that they hadn't returned and sent out a search party.

And there was no guarantee that such a prime target as a group of wounded beastmen wouldn't be attacked by wild beasts or monsters in the meanwhile.

To avoid this, it was critical the two of them remain in good health. That way, he could send the youth back to the camp for aid, while he used every ounce of his power to heal and protect the injured from monsters, until help could arrive.

Of course, who knew if things would even proceed that well. Perhaps the humans didn't care whether a war started and would try to kill them anyway. The beastmen were the first to attack, after all, so they could easily claim self-defense. There was a strong chance that the other beastmen, not wishing for a war with the humans, would retreat.

However, they were running out of options.

For now, only the mage and the youth were in any shape to talk. And since he outranked the youth, the mage was currently in charge.

So, the mage shouted, in a loud and determined voice, "We surrender! Please don't kill us!"

"Now then, what shall we do? It would be too much work to bring all of them along," Reina said, pondering.

"Wouldn't it be better to kill them?" Pauline asked nonchalantly.

A shiver ran through the restrained beastmen.

Of course, she wasn't being serious; she was bluffing so the men wouldn't take them lightly. And to have a bit of fun, too.

"Please wait!" The hasty protest came not from the beastmen but from the leader of the escort hunters.

"That would be a mistake before we understand what the whole situation is," the man said. "If this goes south, it could mean conflict with the beastpeople as a whole. Let's try and handle this a little more gently."

Apparently, he had thought his new allies were being serious.

"Hm, I wonder. Guess it depends if they answer us truthfully when we question them," Reina said.

However, in spite of the ample threat Reina and Pauline represented, the beastmen's lips were sealed. Despite lengthy questioning from a number of angles, they gave not a single answer, not for why they had captured the investigation team and the hunters, nor for what they were doing at that worksite.

Well, at any rate, it didn't take a genius to figure out the beastmen had captured the humans to prevent them from finding out what they were doing at the site.

As they couldn't rightly torture them, everyone was growing a bit frazzled. That was when Mile butted in.

"What exactly do you hope to do by excavating something like that after all this time? I'm sure it's because those people asked you to, but you realize you're only being used, don't you?"

"What?! H-how do you know about it? And they would never—"

The youth fell straight into Mile's trap.

"Y-you idiot! Quit talking!!" the leader screamed.

Mile grinned. She had confirmed nothing more than what Dr. Clairia had theorized, but that meant any information they did get would now be significantly more reliable. Their motives were still unclear, but at least now they were certain of the beast-people's goal.

"We aren't going to get anything more out of them without torturing them," said Mile.

"That's true. Shall we kill them?" Reina asked lightly.

"Oi oi oi oi oi oi oi oi!!!"

As the group interjected, Reina scowled. "That was obviously a joke!"

However, a singular sentiment rang in everyone's hearts:

It sure didn't sound that way!!!

The beastmen, meanwhile, were pale and trembling.

"Truthfully, I'd like to take along two or three of them," said the escort leader, looking the beastmen's way. "However, if a rescue team comes after them, and they think humans took their allies captive, it's gonna start a big hubbub among the beastpeople."

"You all get that too, don't you?" he continued, glaring at the beastmen. "After we've worked so hard to make peace between humans and beastpeople, this might start conflict all over again! If it does, a lot of folks will die. Hundreds, thousands of people. Women and children. And it'll be all your faults! That's right, you'll be killers of humans and beastpeople, women and children! Is that what you're after, you warmongering idiots?!"

Beastpeople's expressions were difficult to read, but in this case their feelings were perfectly clear. They were stunned, confused, guilty, and a bit offended.

"You're wrong! We would never want to do anything like," a young beastman started, but their leader cut across him.

"Shut up," he snapped. "Don't say another word! I order you as your commander. From now on, no one speaks to the humans without my permission or the elder's!"

Naturally, the clan elder would only get involved if the leader didn't make it home alive. If he didn't, his subordinates wouldn't talk to humans for the rest of their lives. Thus was the authority of their leader's commands when they operated as a team or pack. As long as that authority extended to the elder, even if they returned and found their elder deceased, they would simply wait until a successor was named and freed them from the leader's order.

Even if their entire clan was annihilated, they wouldn't be free from the order. Not unless they integrated with another clan and *that* clan's elder released them from the order. The binding effect of the leader's words was that strong.

"Ah..." The leader of the escort hunters slumped in disappointment.

"It's no use. These guys aren't gonna say another word," Reina said. "Even if we torture them, once it gets to be too much, they'll probably kill themselves."

"Whaaat?! Are you serious?!"

"There's nothing we can do. That's just how beastpeople are!" As much as Reina might protest, this didn't seem like it would pan out in their favor.

"Let's leave 'em all here," said the escort leader.

"Whaaaaaaaat?!?!" The Crimson Vow were floored.

They had gone through the trouble of capturing them, and they were a valuable source of information. It was obvious they should take at least two or three of them back to the capital as prisoners. It might even have a favorable influence on their compensation.

"B-but why?! We should take some of them if we can. At the very least, one," Pauline complained.

However, the leader would not budge.

"You're saying you want to bring this whole bunch of uncooperative beastmen along all the way to the capital?" he asked. "That's going to be a whole heap of trouble in and of itself, as I already said."

"Because of rescuers, false accusations, or a dispute?" asked Mile.

"Yeah, exactly." The leader nodded. "They aren't going to say anything anyway. And if they kill themselves, who's going to take responsibility? Will you?"

"Er..."

The Crimson Vow were out of arguments. They valued their own hides, after all, and couldn't bear that responsibility.

"P-please wait a minute!" they said before separating themselves from the rest of the group. They launched into hushed conversation...

"Sorry to keep you all waiting!"

Several minutes had gone by. The Crimson Vow finally finished their conference and returned to the others.

"All right, we agree to leave all of the beastmen here, alive," said Mile, representing the group.

A sense of relief rippled through the escorting hunters, Tiffy, the guild employee, and the beastmen. Apparently, their conversation had been a little concerning to the nine other hunters, as well as Dr. Clairia and her assistant.

"By the way, Mr. Beastman," Mile stated, addressing their leader. The others were forbidden to speak, so she had no other option. "Am I right to believe you are as eager to avoid conflict as we are?"

The leader nodded.

"In that case, please vacate the dig site before any human troops arrive and put everything back in its place. The local lord might make a fuss about 'trespassers' in his territory, but that's nothing to worry about. How soon do you think you'll be able to pack up and leave?"

"...No idea."

"Huh?" Mile was perplexed by the leader's reply.

"Nothing we can do about it. If we find something, who

knows how long they'll want to keep searching. If we don't find anything, who knows how long it'll be before everyone finally gives up and leaves. Nothing's been decided, either way, and we haven't been given further instructions..."

"Ah..."

Perhaps because he understood Mile and the others wished to avoid conflict, the leader of the beastmen had let a bit of information slip, but it wasn't much of a treat to hear.

"Guess there's no choice. Reina, Pauline, I'll leave the bone breaking to you."

The two of them nodded and approached the restrained beastmen.

And then...

Snap!

"Gaaaaaaaaaaah!!!"

Snap!

"Gwaaaaah!!"

The task that Mile had requested was underway.

...Indeed, the "bone-breaking" task.

Primarily, their legs.

"Wh-wh-what are you doing?!?!" the beastmen's leader screamed in panic.

A sense of calm had overtaken him when he saw a little girl of the same mind had taken charge. That calm had shattered when he saw an unthinkable deed being performed under that same little girl's orders.

"Well, I did say 'bone-breaking.'"

"N-not that! I mean, yes, that, but that's not the point!!!"

Mile stared at him, not understanding his angle.

"Huh? Well, I figured," she said as if this were all perfectly normal, "if you could get everyone to withdraw quickly, we would let you go back right away. But since that won't be possible, then it makes sense to delay you from getting information to your allies for as long as possible. So I'm having them break your legs to slow you down."

The beastmen looked aghast.

"Eek... St-sto...!"

Snap!

"Gaaaaaaah!"

In this world, there was a little thing called healing magic. If there weren't, Mile wouldn't have concocted such a ghoulish scheme. There were aftereffects to such injuries. If you were poor and had to recuperate on your own, a clean break or simple bone fracture came with a strong chance of recovery but not a guaranteed one. There could be lasting joint problems and the like. However, with recovery magic, there was almost no worry at all. And there *was* a mage amongst the beastmen.

Drag...

"Hm?"

Drag drag drag...

"Huhhhhh?"

As Mile grabbed the beastman mage by the collar, he screwed his eyes shut, sure his turn was next, and preparing himself for the pain. But when he had been dragged a short stretch away, he heard a suspicious phrase.

"Fire Wall."

"Wh—?! Eddies of magic, surge forth and defend me! Magic Shield!'"

Hearing Mile let off an attack spell, skipping any incantation, the mage conjured a shield with a brief and hurried spell. This method prioritized speed over efficiency. Some mages could cast powerful spells silently or with no incantation at all, but that was too high a hurdle for this mage. So he put his all into this short incantation.

Because Mile had so leisurely cast her spell, the wall of flame was intercepted by the shield and didn't reach the mage. However, it continued around him, forcing the mage to continue casting his spell. He would have to keep this up until Mile's magic ran out, whenever that was...

Both the mage and his leader knew exactly what she was trying to do.

If the mage still had sufficient magical strength, he could use healing magic. And, if he did, he could channel all that strength into healing at least one of the beastmen and sending him off as a messenger. After that, the mage could rest a while and then heal the rest of his allies.

Even if a monster came their way, between the mage and whoever had been healed so far, they should be able to defend themselves. Plus, having one leg broken wasn't enough to sap beastpeople of their battle strength.

It would only buy them a little time, but a little was better than nothing. It was best to delay the beastmen as long as possible.

It was for that reason Mile intended to drain the mage of all his magic.

"G-g-guhh..."

Mile drew her gaze away from the agonized mage to see Reina and Pauline had already finished off the rest of the beastmen. They grinned, looking incredibly pleased with themselves.

Incidentally, Mavis had refused to participate. She had protested, saying that for someone with aspirations of being a knight, harming an unresisting opponent was unspeakable. Reina had ended the matter with a simple "Oh, no worries," and the matter was quickly settled before proceeding without her.

It would have been better to force Mavis to participate, in order to harden her heart, but Reina wasn't ready to be that hard on her.

"Y-you 'humans'..." the leader moaned bitterly.

The other beastmen were still forbidden to speak and couldn't voice their complaints.

The way he said "humans" clearly implied he thought them more vicious than devils. Because no beastman would ever use "beast" as an insult.

"Since it's just one of your legs, you should be better in no time, right?" Mile said. "The bone hasn't broken the skin, so there won't be any blood. As long as you don't let anything know you're injured, I don't think any monsters would dare to come and attack this many of you. Now then, best of luck!"

After that, Mile pressed the others to make their preparations to depart, and soon after, the whole group left—leaving the twelve broken beastmen where they lay.

Of course, they didn't forget to rescue the mage, who—his magic spent—was about to be consumed in flames, before they departed.

Nor did they forget to break one of his legs...

"...Damn those little devil girls!" the leader of the beastmen spat, although even he was aware that in this incident, they were the ones who were completely in the wrong.

They had willfully invaded human territory and begun an excavation without permission. On top of that, they had abducted and unlawfully held private citizens. Even those girls had only taken on the monumental task of finding and rescuing the investigation team, which the beastpeople had resisted with all their might. Just as the girls had said, they were behaving no differently from bandits.

Of course, they hadn't had violent intentions and doing anything even remotely bandit-like to their captives was the furthest thing from their minds. However, that meant nothing to the captured humans. As far as they were concerned, the beastmen *were* as good as bandits.

Indeed, if they were bandits, they wouldn't be able to complain if the humans *had* decided to kill them. In fact, they should thank those girls for letting them off with a broken leg apiece.

There were also broken arms and ribs from being struck with

the flat of a sword, but those were easily fixed with healing magic. So they couldn't truly be angry about those injuries.

The beastmen's intentions were to do nothing that would bring shame upon their kind, so they tried to do nothing that would harm their people's pride. Or so the leader had said to his subordinates and tried to believe himself. In truth, he was conflicted.

There was a bigger problem at hand, though: They had failed *and* lost to four human girls who were barely even of age.

However, they had more pressing matters to consider for now.

"Bones, get as much rest as you can," the leader commanded the mage. "You need to recover your magic as soon as possible. If you can't use your healing magic, we'll be screwed!"

"Y-yes, sir. Of course, sir," the other replied.

The real problems would come *after* his magic had recovered.

Do I send whoever's leg heals up first as the messenger? What if we're attacked by monsters or wild animals? Can someone who can barely move make it through? I guess I could have the first few stay to defend the rest and send the fourth man... No, that will delay communication by a day. What should I do...?

Thanks to the girls, who had so conscientiously broken Bones' leg as well, the men were not left in the unfortunate circumstance of having him be the only able body, forced to end him off with some remark like, "Don't worry about us, just go and tell them ASAP!" It would have been a hard call and one the leader would have to make. But at least the option would have been there.

Even if he regretted it for the rest of his life...

Did they have that in mind when they broke Bones' leg? So I wouldn't have to be troubled by it...? No! That's impossible! Little girls would never show beastmen such consideration. They just wanted to make sure all our legs were broken. There couldn't be any other reason.

As he thought this, the leader was suddenly reminded of the somewhat-vapid little girl and her unhinged smile.

He couldn't help but worry. Beastpeople were, by nature, captivated by the strong. And for the sake of their young, they harbored strong, protective instincts. It was only natural that he should feel concern for Mile and Reina.

For Mavis and Pauline? Adults could fend for themselves, so there was no point in worrying over anyone who had already chosen a companion.

Mile, of course, hadn't thought about it either way.

When she had released the mage from the fire wall, she noticed there was a leg that hadn't been broken and took care of it on reflex.

That was all there was to it.

Why did she break his leg?

Because it was there.

Didn't I Say to Make My Abilities *Average* in the Next Life?!

CHAPTER 31 |

To the Capital

THE CRIMSON VOW and the eighteen rescued humans made it safely through the forest and onto the main road leading to the regional capital.

Though it was called the main road, it was a small country road, just wide enough for a single cart. Two carts couldn't pass each other except in the designated pull-off spaces placed here and there for that specific purpose.

Just as they had planned, the group didn't stop in at the village at the edge of the woods. They no longer had to worry about the beastpeople's retrieval team, but they had wasted more time than they anticipated on questioning, and if they stopped in town, it was unlikely they would make it to the capital before dark. Not a single person objected.

"If only we'd had prisoners, *if only we'd had prisoners*, the reward would..." Pauline sighed.

"Oh, be quiet," the guard leader yelled. "I already told you, I'll make sure they know you all *did* take prisoners, and *we* were the ones who decided to let them go! We got a bit of information, so we can use that as a bargaining chip to raise your reward a bit! That should be fine, right, Miss Guild Employee?!"

Tiffy jolted. "Y-yes, I will give my endorsement as well!"

The guard leader, worn down by Pauline's incessant, obstinate complaints, finally snapped. He hoped the offer was more than a baseless promise. He wondered what might have happened if his opinion wasn't well received and suddenly recalled Pauline's gleeful face as she broke the beastmen's legs. He shuddered.

"By the way, Doctor, " Mile suddenly began. Dr. Clairia looked her way.

"Yes~?" Clairia replied.

"D-do you happen to know a woman from the capital branch of the Hunter's Guild named Theresa?"

"Ah..." Clairia made an amused but slightly weary face. "I'm not sure how many times I've been asked this. A lot of people assume her to be an elf or half-elf because of her youthful appearance, but both her parents are completely human. Well, I mean, maybe there's *some* elf blood somewhere way back in the family line and a recessive trait just reared its head. That's not impossible. But, as far as I know, she's a perfectly normal human."

"Whaaaaaaat?!"

There was a cry of shock from not only the Crimson Vow, but

Tiffy and the guard hunters, as well. Apparently, Theresa was well known around these parts.

Tiffy was flabbergasted. "Since it's a taboo in the guild to pester other hunters about their personal details, no one had the nerve to actually ask her. We all just assumed she was an elf or half-elf or something..."

The secret to maintaining a youthful appearance was worth its weight in gold, especially for women. If it was just a matter of elven blood, the matter could be easily abandoned. But when it was a human who managed it, well, that was when jealousy arose.

Apparently, they had stepped on a land mine.

The city of Helmont wasn't so far from the royal capital. The five days' distance between them was considered "relatively short." Plus, it was the capital; it wouldn't be strange to see information be exchanged between guild employees.

"That woman..."

Growing frightened of Tiffy, who stared at the ground grumbling, Mile and the others hurriedly gave her some space.

The party managed to arrive in Helmont before the sun set for the evening. They headed straight for the guildhall.

A few hunters who saw them along the way rushed to the guildhall ahead of them, kicking up a fuss. They were likely acquaintances of Tiffy, the guards, or the other rescued hunters.

When they finally arrived...

"T-Tiffyyyyyyyyyyy!"

The guild master, who had been waiting in front of the

building, ran toward them, arms flung wide. His face was soaked
with snot and tears.

"Tiffyyy!"

Before he could embrace her, Tiffy stepped aside. Half-blind
from tears, he continued rushing forth and eventually wrapped
his arms tight around Clairia.

"Gaaaaaaaaaaaaaaaaaaaaaaaah!!!"

"...And that's the sum of it," Mile concluded.

The guild master gave an emphatic nod, both cheeks bright
red and covered in stark scratch marks.

It was intensely undignified.

Mile was the one talking because this was their job completion
report and she was the best-equipped to tell the story. When it
came to most things, the others treated Mile's mindset as somewhat
unfortunate at best, but even they were aware that when it came to
recalling and delivering facts, Mile was far superior to them.

The investigation team would give their report once all matters with the Crimson Vow were settled and the girls had returned home.

"After this, I'll take the report from the investigation team,"
the guild master explained. "Then I'll send my report over to the
lord's estate. Compensation will be settled then, so please come
back tomorrow. We can't thank you girls enough, and we'll never
forget what you've done."

What he wished to say was, "Thank you for saving my daughter," but now he spoke as the guild master. He had to be mindful of the ceremony expected of him.

The Crimson Vow, recognizing this, nodded and left the conference room.

"Guess it's over."

"That's the end of it."

The entire investigation team had been brought back alive, which was something the client probably hadn't expected. They had also rescued nearly half of the other missing hunters (the rest had probably fallen victim to unruly monsters who had been forced from their territories, so bringing back half, safe and sound, was quite an achievement).

It was an impressive, unexpected success. Even Mavis and Pauline couldn't help grinning in satisfaction.

"Now then, for dinner tonight," Reina proposed. "Let's pay them triple the rate and have them cook us up something special. Sound good?"

"Yeah!!!"

Reina's proposal was unanimously well received.

The next morning, the Crimson Vow headed for the guildhall right at the first morning bell. It went without saying that they were there to collect their payment. Once they collected what was owed, they planned to turn on the spot and head straight for home in the capital.

When they reached the reception counter, the exchange proceeded normally. "Here is your reward for rescuing the investigation team," the receptionist said while processing their payment, "your reward for uncovering the source of the change in the monsters' habitats, and a bonus for rescuing Dr. Clairia. Plus, while it isn't much, you've been awarded a bonus from the Hunters' Benefit Society for rescuing those nine other hunters and an additional sum as thanks from the hunters themselves."

"You can give that last part back to the other hunters. I'm sure they're in a bind after losing their gear," said Reina, to which Pauline nodded in agreement.

Seeing Pauline, the group miser, go along with this, had Mile reeling in shock.

Wh-what is going on?! They say that the only thing that would get TV Tokyo to interrupt its usual broadcast for a special report would be the end of the world, but this is way bigger than that!!!

TV Tokyo was a remarkable television station that, even on the brink of the Gulf War or impending natural disasters, had perpetually refused to deviate from its scheduled programming. Also known as the western SUN-TV or East TV Tokyo, they were pioneers—nay, *heroes*—in the world of television, the pride of Japan. In her previous life, Mile had been a firm devotee.

"No, that won't do," the receptionist explained. "If we make an exception here, others will start hesitating to pay the reward, citing you all as an example. If that happens, you'll start seeing all sorts of absurd situations, such as people refusing to save others when they figure out that the victims have no intention of paying a reward or delaying helping until payment is confirmed..."

Reina looked a little taken aback, but understood. "Well, guess we better take it then."

"Including your compensation for releasing the prisoners you took on the investigation team's orders, and the reward for the intelligence you gathered, this is the final amount."

The receptionist placed a leather sack atop the counter with a resounding *thud*.

"Whooooooaaa!!!"

The four of them shouted in shock, their eyes wide. The reward was far greater than they had expected. There couldn't just be silver or copper pieces inside.

"The guild master requested you stop by his office, as there's something he'd like to discuss with you. So, if you all would," the receptionist directed.

Thinking the guild master wanted to give them an additional reward for saving his daughter, or that he wanted to discuss the particulars of their payment, the four proceeded to his office with a spring in their steps. When they entered the room, the guild master and Dr. Clairia greeted them.

"We'd like you all to go back to the beastmen's camp," the guild master said without introduction. "It's a direct request from our lord."

"Huhh???"

The four of them stood there, shocked at the sudden request. The guild master continued.

"We sent a messenger out to the Capital this morning with a report. A forward rider went ahead as a herald, with a messenger behind them in a carriage. The lord's own subordinates, along with the entire investigation team outside of Dr. Clairia, will be traveling with them."

"But the escort party's weapons..." Mile started.

"The guild lent them some free of charge. They *might* be returned once they get back."

"Oh, I see..." Mile was relieved at the guild master's reply.

To prevent the spread of information, it was reasonable to take the rescued hunters along as both witnesses and guards. Plus, this would help the hunters, whose very livelihood was threatened without their gear. More likely than not, it had been ordered by the guild master, who would have considered that. Although having to return the weapons once they came back was probably quite the bummer.

"Should you make an enemy of the beastpeople, or should the beastpeople begin moving in any sort of organized fashion, and things go sour, there's a chance relations between us will deteriorate as a whole. In the worst case, we may return to a state of public enmity with the beastpeople. You understand this, yes?"

The four of them nodded.

"We cannot prompt the lord of this region to make any careless decisions. Not without approval from the Crown... However, we also can't afford to overlook the mysterious activities of these beastpeople who have invaded our territory. Bringing an envoy from the capital would be an empty gambit, and without knowing their intentions, there's no telling what they will do next. Also..."

"Also?"

"The lord desires whatever treasures they may have unearthed."

"Ah..."

The four understood *exactly* what was going on.

Didn't I Say to Make My Abilities *Average* in the Next Life?!

CHAPTER 32 |

Once More
into the Forest

"Our lord really isn't such a bad person. Well, I suppose he is as prideful and self-important as any other noble, but he does value the safety of his people."

As Mile listened to the guild master, she thought, *What you're saying is, he's really just caring for his prized livestock. So they'll grow up fat and healthy, and give him lots of milk.*

Of course, she would *never* say such a thing out loud.

"For the sake of the management and development of these lands, as well as his own luxury, he is rather stin… gree… *ambitious* when it comes to money."

The four girls were starting to suspect the guild master *wasn't* so fond of the man.

"Anyway, you were personally requested for this job. You know where the beastmen are, you've already infiltrated and escaped the place, and even if you're attacked, you have the strength to make it home alive."

Receiving a personal job request from a lord was one of the highest honors a hunter could receive. It was a recognition of their abilities and a mark of confidence in their success. Only a personal request from the king or another member of the royal family would be a higher honor.

Had they been normal hunters, they would have been over the moon and accepted the job without a second thought.

However, they were *not* normal hunters.

"So, what does he want us to do?" Reina asked coldly.

"He wants you to confirm the status of the beastmen, confirm what they're excavating, and, if possible, reclaim it."

"..."

The four said nothing. Mile eventually broke the silence.

"Um, may I ask you something?"

"Sure," the guild master replied.

"I think that counts as looting. Wouldn't that make us thieves?"

"Uh..." The guild master stared dumbly. "Well, n-no, that land is part of our country's territory, so..."

"But that doesn't mean we control it, does it? It's just part of the forest. And, generally, whatever someone harvests or hunts out there belongs to them, doesn't it? In that case, whatever the beastmen find is *theirs*, and not ours, right?

"Obviously, kidnapping hunters is a criminal act, but until we get a missive from the capital, we can't protest it or request that the parties at fault turn themselves over, can we? And *other* beastpeople doing some gathering isn't a problem, is it? Wouldn't pillaging their site be a criminal act on *our* part?"

"..."

Stealing underground resources of another country on your own country's orders would be an enormous problem, perhaps even a diplomatic conflict. However, there was little issue with a group of private citizens doing a bit of small-scale gathering or treasure hunting on their own in foreign lands. If such a thing were forbidden, then hunters—whose activities already blurred national lines—would never be able to make a career.

While the beastmen had in fact started some kind of large-scale operation, they were "digging in order to find something," and that didn't count as a large-scale mining operation for resources. Therefore, if they were to seize whatever (probably minuscule) materials the beastpeople ended up uncovering, then who was the real villain here?

"I-I suppose that's true..." Having this pointed out, the guild master's words suddenly left a bad taste in his mouth.

"Mind if we discuss this amongst ourselves?" asked Mile.

The guild master gave his consent, and the four girls moved to the adjoining conference room.

Several minutes later, they returned, once again taking their seats in the guild master's office.

"We discussed it, and we've decided to take the job," said Mile.

The guild master looked relieved. Turning down a personal request from a lord was unheard of. This branch would become the laughing stock of the hunter's guild, never mind the blow to the lord's reputation and temper. Rumors about the "incompetent and unreliable branch that couldn't even convince a group of rookie hunters to take on a lord's personal request" would begin to spread far and wide, from the capital to the farthest reaches of the land.

"However, as long as there is no sufficient reason to do so, we will not reclaim the item. The original request was phrased 'should the possibility arise,' so I don't believe that will be an issue."

What counted as "sufficient reason," the four had decided, was if the object turned out to be something dangerous or something they couldn't allow to be handed over to the beastmen or their allies.

Mile, of course, had read plenty of fantasy novels and had already taken into consideration that such tropes as that they might be digging in the hopes of "reviving a demon king" or "breaking the seal on the prison of an evil god." Of course, so had Mavis, Reina, and Pauline, since they had listened to Mile's strange tales for nearly a year.

Part of the reason they decided to take the job was the points a personal request from a lord would net them. It was too tempting for their eventual B-rank promotion and would be a huge boost to their reputation, besides. But mostly, they were worried. If they refused the job, it would be given to some other party, and that party might go missing again or come to blows with the beastmen. Which could easily blow up into a huge incident.

Plus, they were keen to retrieve the other hunters' confiscated gear and return it to them.

Were they being too kind? Or were they underestimating the job?

Well, that was just the way the Crimson Vow was.

"Y-yeah, of course, that's not a problem. I mean, I'm sure our lord didn't really think four little girl rookie hunters would be capable of stealing back any treasure in the first place. That's probably why it came with the provision of, 'should the opportunity arise.'"

The guild master was relieved the negotiations were settled, but he suddenly realized he had neglected one last important detail.

"Oh, by the way, Dr. Clairia will be accompanying you, so I'll also have to ask you to put your all into guarding her."

"Wh-what the heck?! You didn't say anything about that!" Reina raged.

Her three companions were completely calm. They had already figured that out. Why else would Dr. Clairia not return to the capital and in fact be sitting in the room right now? Unfortunately, Reina was the only one who had yet to figure it out.

There was nothing strange about a scholar accompanying them to investigate a dig site and an artifact, after all. It was, however, perhaps not the best idea to expose Dr. Clairia—an elf, a scholar, and more than likely a person of note—to such danger. Given that she *had* been part of the initial investigation team, though, she was probably more concerned with investigation and research than with the dangers that might accompany them.

"The lord will also be sending out some reinforcements,

though it seems like that's still in the works. They'll probably be heading out after you've already left."

There was no way of knowing if these men were actual reinforcements or observers, making sure the Crimson Vow didn't make off with any treasure. The words "barrier troops" floated through their minds.

"I guess that might be useful. So, how many troops is he sending out?" asked Reina.

The guild master answered, sourly, "One."

"What?!"

"You heard me. Just one."

That settled it. This person would be there as a watchman. They might get in the way, but they probably wouldn't be very useful.

If anything happened to the Crimson Vow, they probably wouldn't even step in to help, merely reporting what had happened to the lord. The girls would far prefer if they weren't around.

The four of them thought the same thing at once: *Let's lose 'em.*

Afterwards, they tossed a few ideas around and finally settled on leaving immediately. They had hoped to take a day to relax, but now, time was of the essence.

By now, thanks to the mage, several of the beastmen were probably recovered enough for combat, even if they weren't yet fully healed. They most certainly had sent word back to the dig site. The dig site, meanwhile, was probably shorthanded and vulnerable. Perhaps they were panicking, since they had learned their allies were crippled out in the woods. They might be hurrying to form a rescue team. The Crimson Vow weren't foolish enough to overlook such important factors, especially when planning an infiltration.

Dr. Clairia had anticipated this as well and finished her preparations the night before.

The Crimson Vow, of course, were always ready to leave at a moment's notice, thanks to Mile and her "storage." Since they had intended to head straight to the capital anyway, they were already checked out of the inn.

"Well then, let's get going!" Reina cried.

"All right!!!" the three companions answered.

Dr. Clairia was just a second behind. "All right!"

"Mavis, here."

A short while after they left town, Mile gently stretched her hand out to Mavis.

"Are these...?"

"Supplements to the other ones. Just in case. If you use them, I can resupply you with more, so please don't hesitate. If you don't try it at least once, you'll be going in blind when the time comes."

"Got it. I'm glad to do so, thank you."

Mavis pulled three of the mysterious little capsules out of the container and placed them in her pocket. She now had five in total.

If she didn't hurry up and try them out soon, Mile would keep offering her more. Soon, her pockets would be bulging. The premonition hung clearly in Mavis's mind.

As was now the norm, Mile and the others skipped over the village on the outskirts of the forest. Thanks to the guidance of Dr. Clairia, who was skilled at moving through the woods, they kept up a brisk pace, traveling much quicker than they had during their escape.

Evening came quickly, the light growing dim within the forest. Once more, Mile attached wood blocks, painted with her humble "magical luminescent material" to each of their backs.

They moved in single file, what in another life Mile would have called a "Jet Stream Attack." Of course, no one would be vaulting off anyone else's head.

Mile, with her sharp night vision, was at the head of the line. Reina, Dr. Clairia, Pauline, and Mavis followed, in that order. Naturally, Clairia, their VIP, was dead center with Pauline, who had the most limited close-range abilities as well as ever-important healing magic. Mavis, of course, was at the tail, prepared to take on anything that might come from the rear. Mages were weak against surprise attacks, after all.

"If they were quick, the messenger will have arrived at the dig site right around now," Mile calculated. "Or not, if they left only a little while ago..."

Considering the physical capabilities and forest-dwelling experience of beastmen, if a messenger moved at top speeds, he could make it to the excavation site within a day. But really, it all came down to that mage's magical recovery speed, his healing capabilities, and whether the leader would favor sending word over the well-being of the team.

"Let's take a detour," Mile said. "If we keep heading straight toward the excavation site, we might run into that team or even a rescue unit. I'd rather avoid that. And there's one other place I would very much like to avoid..."

The Crimson Vow didn't know what other place Mile referred to, but because it was Mile who was saying so, they consented without much question.

"...Erk!"

It had only been a day since they entered the forest. They were very near the dig site, when suddenly, Dr. Clairia stopped in place. She covered her nose and mouth.

"What's wrong? Oh no, elves have a sharper sense of smell than humans, don't they? Everyone, change course immediately! This is 'the forbidden place!'"

"I suspected something like this," Reina said wearily. "When you had us take that early break so close to that pile of dung, and the beastmen chasing us ended up being *much* slower than expected..."

Pauline and Mavis nodded in agreement.

Even though they had already changed course quite a bit, the smell ranged so far that they had to detour even further. Mile had had in mind that the place might become something of a safe zone—somewhere no monsters or wild animals might wander into—but it had already become so toxic no one could possibly take refuge in it.

The beastmen would most likely detour around the opposite side of the area. Given the sensitivity of their noses, the team with the broken bones would probably take an even bigger detour than the girls. There was no sign of them passing through, such as broken branches, bent grass, or footprints. So they were very certain they would pass through on the other side.

Now a day and a half since leaving the capital—and a full day since entering the forest proper—the Crimson Vow and Dr. Clairia made it safely to the excavation site. There wasn't a beastman in sight.

"We've been powering through for a day and a half with only a short break. Let's take it easy and get some rest tonight," Reina said.

With nothing pinged through Mile's detection magic, they all nodded. It was already growing dark around them.

Mile picked a level patch of grass and pulled a tent from her inventory. Not a folded tent, but an already assembled one. It was an idea that had occurred to her two nights ago. Why waste time assembling and dissembling the tent when she could stash it fully assembled? So the morning before last, when they were packing to go, she put the tent away without folding it, when the others weren't looking.

The sight stopped Dr. Clairia in her tracks. "Wh…?"

The other three paid it no mind, going about their tasks of staking the tent's four corners and digging a drainage ditch around their camp site as though nothing had happened. Even if the weather deteriorated quickly, it was unlikely they would be rained on very hard, given the thick canopy, but it was better to be prepared. That was the secret to a long and healthy life.

"Wh-why wasn't it folded up?!" Dr. Clairia demanded.

"Hm? I mean, it's annoying to have to fold it down and pitch it every single time. It's a waste of time, don't you think?"

Dr. Clairia was dumbfounded.

Typically, the storage capacity of a mage's storage magic was limited by weight and volume. No matter how light an object was, if it had a large volume then the storage space would reach capacity much quicker. If an object was compact but dense, storage would be pushed to its limits all the same. The limit was decided by a combination of these factors, not separately.

It was standard practice to store only objects that were as small and light as possible in storage. Even when within the limits, the more a mage stored, the more magical energy and mental stamina it took to maintain the magic.

And yet, this little girl had decided to skimp on the paltry amount of time it would take to fold and set up a tent—which would reduce its volume greatly—and simply stored it *as is*.

Just how much magical power did she have?! What intense levels of unconscious control went on in that tiny skull?!

Granted, the items she produced during their escape, such as fruit and vegetables that appeared to be fresh from the market and orc meat that appeared recently butchered, were already quite peculiar.

And there was the matter of the wooden weapons she had

suddenly offered the group, the fact she could see in the dark, and her shining wood blocks. She also had the physical strength to ward off a dozen beastmen as though they were nothing...

Clairia's elven intuition gave her the sense Mile was also an elf, just like her. Even if told otherwise, Clairia couldn't help but feel she was unarguably elf-like.

Part of the reason the scholar had come along with the Crimson Vow was that she had a scholarly interest in finding out what the beastmen were up to and seeing for herself what they might excavate. However, since their escape, the professor had found herself inexorably drawn to the girl, transfixed by her mysterious appeal. Thus, she had taken on this dangerous job for the sole purpose of solving the mystery that was Mile.

It was against the hunter's code to ask about the past and abilities of another hunter. Dr. Clairia was aware of this, so she restrained herself from asking directly.

However, it still concerned her. It *bothered* her. *Oh*, how it bothered her. She was about ready to burst!

"Aaaaaaarrrgh!!!"

"Wh-whatever is the matter, Doctor?!" Mile rushed over at Clairia's sudden scream.

"N-nothing at all!"

She feigned serenity, glaring at Mile all the while.

Mile stretched a cord around the outside of the tent and then fastened pieces of metal and wood to each section in pairs of two. These were "alarm clappers."

Until now, whenever they slept outdoors together, Mile had erected a barrier or used her surveillance magic. However, if she became negligent, or moved away from the others, then things could go south. Realizing this, Mile concocted an alarm system that would be effective even without her.

Plus, they had Dr. Clairia with them. She couldn't use such alarming magic in front of the professor, Mile concluded.

Because they had had nothing to eat but preserved rations nibbled during their short breaks, dinner that evening was a proper meal with a number of peculiarly fresh ingredients from Mile's inventory.

Dr. Clairia was concerned as to whether it was safe to cook so close to the beastpeople's site, but Mile reassured her.

"I take care to draw in and contain smoke and scent particles with magic, so it should be fine. Look, this is what they look like all gathered up."

"..."

Mile pointed towards a strange, blackish blob, as Clairia stared in awed silence.

"Time for tonight's Japanese Folktale!"

Just as it always was on the days when they needed to sleep early.

"...And so, the thief, having felled the evil count, left the princess, the old man, and the faithful dog behind. Afterwards, a guard came rushing to the scene of the crime and said to the princess, 'That rascal has stolen something inconceivable... Your underwear!'"

Pfft!

The other girls of the Crimson Vow listened gleefully, but Dr. Clairia sprayed the soup she had been sipping from her nose and mouth. Nostrils stinging terribly, she collapsed in a heap.

Because they had turned in early the night before, they awoke bright and early the next morning.

It was still not quite light when they roused. They ate a quick breakfast of dried foods, completed their morning preparations, stowed their blankets inside the tent, and then merrily went on their way.

"There's a bit of a rise over there, so we should be able to see out over the whole dig..."

"*Oh.*" A quiet word from Mavis interrupted Mile's proposal.

"What's the matter?" Mile asked.

"M-my foot just broke through something..." Mavis replied, her face twitching.

Hearing this, Mile made a break for the small incline, quickly falling to a crouch and looking out over the dig site. As she did, she saw beastmen flooding from one of the huts, kicking up some sort of ruckus.

"It seems like they've got some kind of warning system set up, too..."

"I-I'm sorry! This is all my fault..." Mavis said apologetically.

However, it was not as though she'd *intended* to trip the wire. None of them had thought there would be an alarm, so it would probably just have been a matter of time.

Mile said as much, assuring Mavis not to worry, but over-earnest Mavis did not seem to be comforted.

But was that pit there the last time...?

Mile's eyes fixed on a hole about seven or eight meters in diameter near the center of the dig site. She didn't remember it. However, when she had observed the site before, it was evening and rather dark. Thinking she had probably overlooked it, she now paid it no mind. Now was not the time to be thinking about such things, after all.

"Let's move! If we fight beastmen in terrain with low visibility or a lot of trees, we'll be at a disadvantage!"

Just as Mile suggested, fighting in heavily wooded areas was a problem when your opponents were nimble beastmen, who were skilled in close-range combat. Using powerful fire magic would be difficult, too.

They wanted to leave their opponents relatively unscathed, and therefore hoped to avoid using fire magic. But if they found themselves outnumbered, it would be back on the table. As long as they didn't *kill* the beastmen, they could be fixed back up with healing magic. They would just have to put up with the pain until they were healed.

Of course, if this went poorly, they would be "assaulting some beastfolk in the middle of scavenging." To connect this to the previous incident and have the situation read as, "We went to reclaim the gear stolen by bandits and were attacked again, so we rightfully defended ourselves," they had to ensure their attacks were only reactionary, should the situation come to blows.

Over and over, Mile pressed this upon them. Reina was exasperated at her insistence, but Dr. Clairia was deeply moved.

"I know you said we were relocating, but *where*?!"

Reina's complaint was well founded. They were cutting straight through the forest. There were only trees behind them. Because they were still at something of an elevation, however, the trees were beginning to thin.

Even so, they could still easily be cornered. Even if they retreated at full speed, they would never move quicker than beastmen through the woods. Save for Mile.

If they kept up, they were sure to be attacked when they were exhausted and negligent. It would be safer to pick a preemptive fight somewhere that would be advantageous for them and then run once they had crushed their opponents.

Plus, if they just ran away like this, it would count as a "failed request" on their record.

"We're going to keep up this way and run down the other side of this hill all the way to there. This is reconnaissance-in-force," Mile said, pointing to the dig site.

Dr. Clairia interjected. "You know, Miss Mile. A reconnaissance-in-force maneuver typically involves slightly reckless action to seek out information about an enemy whose location you're already aware of or making a move that they can't ignore in order to stir them up and gauge their general disposition. At the very least, it doesn't usually mean storming the enemy stronghold and gathering information *after* everyone has been defeated. Are you sure you aren't thinking of a *disruption*-in-force?"

"I-I know that much! I watched a video about the 'craft of war,'" Mile snapped back, perturbed.

"'Vee-dee-oh'? 'Orc raft?'"

Dr. Clairia clearly couldn't follow her Terran terminology. Then again, even if she had used words from this world to explain it, such as "combat tactics" or "digital film record," the point still wouldn't have gotten across.

In any case, there was no time. There was no telling how soon they would end up surrounded, so they didn't have the luxury of a leisurely debate.

"No use. I don't think it's a *good* plan, but since I can't think of a better one, process of elimination means Mile's plan is the best. Let's just try to make sure non-combatants get a chance to escape unharmed."

With Reina's approval, their course of action was cemented.

"All right, let's do it!"

"All right!!!" the other three cheered.

"...All right!" As always, Dr. Clairia was just one beat behind.

They rushed the enemy camp but without shout or battle cry.

Until they were discovered, they would remain in the shadows, forging forward in silence. Then they would lie in wait just before one of the open areas. Their scent would eventually give them away, but there was no sense in hastening the inevitable.

Naturally, the beastpeople must know where their alarm system had been triggered, so they could expect them to surround and approach, trying to block their escape route. They probably didn't expect a small group to be coming their way, so when they got to where they expected the girls to be, only to find no one there, they would probably panic and start gaining on them.

For Mile and the others, this would mean they had been chased down by an attacking enemy, and driven into their camp, and not that they had infiltrated the camp of their own volition. By extension, any mayhem, injuries, or property and artifact damage would be because the beastmen came at them, absolving the party of even a modicum of blame.

Then, they could gather more information during the confusion or proceed once they had driven the beastmen away. There was a chance that whatever they were searching for might be destroyed or lost in the fray, but that wasn't the girls' problem. In fact, it might just be better if the item went "missing" during the battle.

"You're always such an airhead, how is this the one area where you've got a bit of sense?!" Reina gave an exasperated shout as Mile explained the plan.

Several minutes later, just as planned, the beastmen had rushed to the point where they thought the intruders were. Seeing no one, nor any signs of them heading back, they were now proceeding back toward the dig site in order to surround the intruders from behind. Since they would likely be following their scents, it was only a matter of time before the girls were discovered.

And then, finally...

"There they are! Surround those intruders and capture them!" shouted one of the beastmen, pointing at the group.

"Oh *no*! The enemy has surrounded us and ordered our capture! We'd better run! I *guess* we're being forced right into this open space!"

Mile stood up and began bolting directly towards the center of the dig site.

"Wah! While running away from the bandits attacking us, we ended up running right into some strange place! Is this the bandits' secret hideout?!" she shouted in a loud and stilted voice.

There were now only ten beastpeople blocking the way ahead of them—all adult males. All of the women and youths had taken refuge in the huts, which, as far as Mile and company were concerned, was a favorable circumstance.

"Intruders shouldn't be sayin' such disrespectful things!"

"And bandits shouldn't be acting so haughty!"

"Wh..."

As long as they didn't know the truth of the matter, the men were as good as bandits. Even if that turned out to not be the case later, they were bandits for now and would be handled accordingly. Honestly, if this incident ended up being of international significance, they would be better off being considered as such.

"What?" Reina interjected. "Are you saying that's wrong? Then what are you all doing here? And why did you capture those hunters and steal their things? Are you going to explain why you're acting *exactly* like bandits?!"

"Er..."

The beastmen, lost for words, didn't reply. Some of them looked like ones who had been present for the previous incident.

"Ugh, shut up! Oi, you lot, capture those girls already! ... What's wrong?"

For beastmen—who had a very strict respect for hierarchy— failure to obey a superior's orders would normally be unthinkable. Mile thought it very suspicious the men didn't act, until she looked more closely at them. Yes, they *were* very familiar...

"Oh! These men are the ones who attacked us!" At Mile's shout, eight men twitched and stiffened.

"What?" the leader shouted. "Are you telling me *these* girls are the lady hunters you said you scared off? Didn't you say there were just four... wait! Isn't that one there one of the prisoners who escaped?! Were they hanging around here this whole time?! The humans still don't know what's going on, then! Wait!! Where are the other seventeen?!"

The girls were under no obligation to answer. The humans had made it back safely, and they could still take precautions to limit the beastpeople's actions, even without new information.

"Damn it, say something! What are you all so afraid of?"

As the leader stared in wonder at his subordinates, who still failed to move, an inconceivable thought crossed his mind.

It was just the other day that his men had returned with their report of the girls.

When they had come seeking healing services, and he had asked why they had so many injuries, they said that in order to ward the intruders off without harming them, they had taken attacks from a mage. But...it couldn't be...

Suspicion bubbled up in his heart, but he couldn't press them in front of the enemy.

However, just in case, he would have to prepare himself. Because, soon, probably very soon... *Gwah!*

Fwooooosh...

"Gwah!"

"Guh-ha!"

A bizarre smell began drifting through the area.

The Crimson Vow's faces contorted as well—just slightly after the beastmen's.

"Th-this smell..."

"Hwahaha! Did you really think someone as brilliant as me was going to go along with your story?! The reserve forces I sent out to lie in wait have finally returned! Now, face our overwhelming battle prowess, and be... *Huuuurk!*"

Apparently, their "battle prowess" had been significantly lowered.

There were fourteen men in front of them, who were huddled up puking. There were twenty at their rear, gaunt and wobbling— and still reeking.

Only the first fourteen still appeared to be in top shape. So, no one could say their battle strength was *improved* with the additional numbers.

The ones who had fallen for the stink trap had probably washed themselves hard, but the smell still hadn't come all the way out. There were even some pitiful forms among them who had shaved their fur, hoping to rid themselves of every trace of the stench.

"M-Mile, what in the world is that...?" Reina asked.

Mavis gasped. "Are you saying *Mile* did this?"

"P-please forgive me..."

Though their noses were nowhere near as sharp as the beastmen's, Reina, Pauline, and Mavis were all on the brink of fainting. As was Mile, whose nose *was* sharper than the average human's.

Dr. Clairia, of course, was on the ground, vomiting.

A shout, from Mile, resounded through the area.

"Waaaaaah!!! Smell, go awaaaay! Destroy all the sources of this smell here and throughout the whole foreeeest!!!"

"*Huff, huff, huff...* Th-thank you so much..."

Though they were enemies, the leader of the beastmen offered Mile his thanks for ridding them of the smell.

"*Hrff, hrff, hrff...* N-no worries, it was my pleasure."

Neither side could be considered in their best form, but there was no time to sit around and chatter; the battle was about to begin.

Before it did, however, Mavis pulled something from her pocket. It was a small, capsule-like vessel: the gift Mile had given her. Because there were so many enemies, she had already decided it was time to use it. She gripped the capsule in her hand and uttered:

"Let's see what you've got, Micross!"

Mile had once described the contents of this object to Mavis. *"Inside this capsule is a very, very tiny object that can restore the power of your 'spirit.' When the going gets tough, please don't hesitate to use it."*

Because this world didn't yet have a word equivalent to "nano," Mile had elected to call it something equivalent to "micro." It was a soup full of microscopic things. "Microsoup," or "Micross" for short. The word that Mavis used was obviously not pronounced the same, but it carried the same meaning.

With this prayer offered to the capsule, Mavis unscrewed the cap and gulped down the liquid.

"True Godspeed Blade EX!"

With Mavis's cry, the battle was underway.

Naturally, Reina and Pauline had already prepared their spells before the fighting even began. This wasn't cowardly; it was no different, actually, than a swordsman gripping the hilt before the fight began.

They let those spells fly before the beastmen could draw nearer. There was no mage in any world who would wait for an enemy skilled in close-range combat to approach them.

"Ultra Super Deluxe Hot Tornado!"

"Gyaaaaaah!!!"

Following Pauline's special non-lethal (if you didn't count souls) hot magic spell, Reina fired her own spell.

"Ultrasonic!"

"Eeeeeeek!!!"

After discussing it with Mavis, who was well aware of Reina's frightening philosophy that "as long as it's non-lethal, friendly fire isn't a problem," Mile had come up with a sort of magic perfect for fighting beastpeople—one that affected only beastpeople and not their allies. She had taught it to Reina before they set out.

Naturally, the ones who had the highest probability of being caught in Reina's attack spells were the frontline fighters. For Mavis and Mile, it was a literal matter of life and death.

What flew out from Reina's spell, though, was an incredibly unpleasant burst of sound, inaudible to humans but perfectly audible to beastmen, who could hear a much wider range of frequencies.

The beastmen clapped their hands over their ears in pain, while the Crimson Vow, who were humans, stood calmly. Almost.

"Gweeehhh..." Mile could feel the bile rising. "St-stop! Stop that speeeeell!"

Her range of hearing was even broader than the beastmen's.

Wh-why? I was perfectly fine when we practiced this.

Mile was utterly perplexed. During their practice sessions, Reina had only been concentrating on projecting the spell forward. Now, though, it was reverberating through the entire area. Plus, she had only timidly attempted this spell when practicing; now, she hurled it at full strength, without limits.

Following the first damaging wave of Reina's spell, Mavis rushed into the twenty men of the original search party who hadn't been struck by Pauline's attack.

I feel so light, Mavis marveled. *My body and my sword feel as light as air!*

In her previous life, Mile would have been able to perfectly name the euphoric feeling Mavis had: *doping.*

Thanks to the microsoup, chock full of nanomachines, the concentration of nanomachines in Mavis's body was now leagues higher than what she would normally possess or even knowingly ingest. And so, if she used her normal "True Godspeed Blade" in her current state...

Once more, Mavis raised her battle cry. "True Godspeed Blade EX!"

That was the most important part, after all.

Mile was lagging behind.

The damage she had taken from Reina's spell was massive. However, as the beastmen had been hurt not only by Reina's spell but also Pauline's, they wouldn't be a problem. Before the beastmen had a chance to get to Reina and Pauline, Mile struck.

No match for Mile's true speed or power, the beastmen fell to the ground, one after another.

Why had she gotten serious now?

Well, there was no telling how many more "non-lethal attack spells" Reina and Pauline would be inclined to use if the battle dragged on.

"It's not like it'll kill anyone, so it's okay if your allies get caught in the fire!" Pauline had once said.

The two of them were of the same mind.

They would, without hesitation, rain down utter annihilation, even upon dear friends. That was Reina and Pauline's way.

They would never be dissuaded or deterred.

Have I surpassed the limits of human ability? Mavis wondered, fighting at full strength just the same.

Like this, she could even best her father or eldest brother in the blink of an eye. She knew that for certain.

No, this isn't really my own strength. The True Godspeed Blade I can summon with my personal spiritual power is, but this power from that special medicine is only temporary. Even so, I will accept it and fight with my full potential! Besides—

Mavis quickly glanced behind her.

—if we don't hurry up and end this, I could end up caught in one of their spells!!

With the same thought weighing on their minds, Mile and Mavis fought for their lives. However desperate, they still refused to strike with full strength. All their nervous reactions were concentrated into controlling their speed and power so as not to cause grave injury.

But then, just as it seemed they were about to achieve victory—and without facing a second wave of spells from Reina and Pauline—*it* appeared.

"Grruurrrrrrrrr..."

Near the center of the dig site was a hole about seven or eight meters in diameter. From within it, something *huge* clambered out.

"A-an earth dragon?" Though shocked, Reina immediately began incanting a spell.

She had initially prepared a non-lethal spell for the beastmen, but such a thing would be of no use against a dragon. She immediately discarded it and began another. Pauline did the same.

Mile and Mavis quickly struck down the remaining beastmen and turned their swords to face the dragon.

"Firebomb!"

"Ultra Hot!"

The two mages fired their spells in tandem, but while Reina's struck the dragon in the gut, it appeared to have no effect. Pauline's spell dissipated before it reached the dragon's head.

"No way..."

"H-how?"

Even for a dragon, taking a direct hit from a firebomb spell—particularly a powerful one—without any damage, or even *flinching*, was unthinkable. And Pauline's spell had simply vanished. Inconceivable!

Seeing the dragon unharmed and continuing to approach them, and that Reina and Pauline were too stunned to prepare more spells, Mile decided to step in herself. This was perhaps the first time she ever needed to use a *serious* attack spell.

"Exploding Magic, Fire!"

Pow!

"Wh..."

The powerful spell, fired in earnest to fell the dragon, was deflected.

As Mile stood, taken aback, the dragon, who had been slowly thudding towards them all the while, moved with a quick and accurate strike, lashing its tail at Mile.

"Gyaaaaaah!!"

Helpless, Mile flew toward the stone ruins ten meters away. Her body crashed into the half-collapsed rubble.

"*Miiiiiile!!!*" Reina, Mavis, and Pauline all shouted. Before they could help her, though, they had to do something about the dragon.

The three tried their hardest to convince themselves it was just like the time with the rock lizard, that she would be fine; it was Mile, after all. Even so, they knew the chances of that prayer being answered were slim.

"Gaaaaaaaah..."

An immense and unbelievable pain coursed all through Mile's body.

Ow ow ow ow owww! What's with this?! That blow wasn't any different from the rock lizard's...

She had never felt such pain, not in her previous life and certainly not since her reincarnation. It was as though every bone in her body were broken... No, they probably *were* broken. Shattered into pieces and now piercing her muscles and internal organs. The pain was all she could think about.

Why? I thought I was supposed to have half the sturdiness of an elder dragon... Why didn't their magic go through...?

The dragon turned to face her. She couldn't move a muscle, nor utter a sound from the horrendous pain, but the dragon continued to approach. It opened its enormous mouth, and...

"Oh? I struck you, and yet you live... Just what are you?"

"I-It spoke?!" Pauline cried, but Reina and Mavis, now realizing what they were truly up against, bit their lips in fear.

"A-an elder dragon..."

Yes. Not an earth dragon but an *elder* dragon, whose power, intelligence, magic, and strength was the greatest in all the world—and of which Mile possessed but half its power...

Fight to the Finish

A-AN ELDER DRAGON…

Thanks to the dragon speaking, Mile now realized the truth as well.

There's no way we can beat it! Elder dragons have twice my strength, twice my magical power, and are smarter than any human! There's no way we could!

For a short time now, she hadn't moved at all. The nanomachines had heard Mile's unconscious cry of distress and were currently in the process of performing an emergency healing, but it would take a bit more time before she was able to move.

If her bones had been merely broken, the healing would have been incredibly fast, perhaps even instantaneous. However, bone fragments had torn her muscles and organs to shreds so repairing her would take that much longer.

The greatest problem of all, though, more painful than broken bones, was that Mile's *heart* was broken.

Since she had first learned of her own strength, Mile hadn't once felt truly in danger. Even up against bandits or powerful monsters, she would think, *If it comes down to it, I just have to get serious. I'll be fine*—and that was true. Therefore, she had always had plenty of leeway and went about her days carefree.

But now, her life was in true, mortal peril. She was up against an elder dragon, an unbeatable foe.

Despair and defeat consumed her.

The wheels in her head were refusing to turn. She couldn't think. As the creature of nightmare approached, prepared to visit death upon her, she could do naught but watch helplessly, paralyzed with unimaginable pain, waiting for the end to come...

"Aaaaaaaaarrrhhh!!!"

As the elder dragon plodded towards Mile, Mavis rushed in. She struck the monster with the literal limits of her power and might.

Thwack!

However, even this mighty blow did nothing more than scratch the dragon's hide.

"Oho, scratched my scales, did you? You're a formidable one. However..." With a swing of its arm, the dragon flicked Mavis away. **"Know your place, whelp!"**

Just like Mile, Mavis was sent crashing into the ruins and collapsed into a heap. Unlike Mile, however, she hadn't taken a powerful blow from the dragon's tail. It had been a mere flick of its hand, so her injuries weren't fatal. Even so, she was in no shape to move.

By then, Reina and Pauline had gotten to their feet and were preparing a second round of spells. Even after seeing what happened to Mavis, they had no intention of stopping.

There were just some things that took priority over others. Now wasn't the time to waste carefully incanted spells or precious seconds on futile things like calling out Mavis's name in worry.

Finally, their spells were complete.

"Blaze, O flames of Hell! Burn my enemies down to the bone!"

If the dragon was going to repel her spell, Reina would just have to surround it. For this, she used an area-attack fire spell, her specialty.

Fwooosh!

"Wh..."

The dragon didn't even look Reina's way. The whorl of flame that was set to envelope the dragon merely vanished, as though it was nothing.

"Rocks, show me your truest form!"

By nature, Pauline wasn't the type of mage to cast a powerful spell or simply pull together an incantation on the spot. So without the blessing of a surplus of time, she couldn't use powerful attack magic.

However, the elder dragon was utterly ignoring both her and

Reina. It had deemed them non-threats, unable to harm it and unworthy of its time.

Therefore, there *was* a spell that Pauline could use.

Judging by what had happened so far, it was clear that any magic would vanish before it struck or deal no damage even if it did. However, Mavis's sword had damaged its scales, even if only to the faintest degree. Thus, this was the only spell she could use.

It was one Mile had devised especially for Pauline, who was weak when it came to combat magic:

"We need to think of a special move for you, Pauline! In case you're in a spot where ice magic, which is your specialty, doesn't have enough physical strength for what you need to do. This is a last-ditch magic, for when your chances of victory and survival are at zero. Let's call this 'Zero-Zero Magic'!"

Mile had taught her rock sculptures weren't made by humans. Rocks held whatever forms were within them all along; humans merely came along and chipped away the excess parts, to reveal what was hidden inside.

Therefore, she just had to request the rock to reveal its true form.

"Zero-Zero Magic No. 1, Rock Reveal!"

Suddenly, rubble began to tumble from a two-meter-high slab amongst the ruins. Bit by bit, its form changed. Beneath the rubble was...

A structure two meters in length. It resembled a spear but was the same thickness from tip to end. It spiraled and twisted, much like a screw.

Were someone from Mile's previous life to view it, there was no doubt they would have uttered to themselves, "Oh, a drill..."

"Turn, turn! As a wagon axle turns, as a cyclone swirls! Use your power, and pierce my enemy! Shoooooot!"

Ka-shunk!

"Graaaaaaaaarrrh!"

Granted ballistic stability from its rotation, just as Pauline directed, the drill shot straight into the elder dragon's flank. The hard and sturdy rock of the ruins withstood the initial shock of striking the dragon's mass. Combined with the kinetic energy of its own mass and the rotational force, it pierced the dragon's scales, buried itself inside, and then shattered.

Even if the section that had been struck was relatively close to the surface, and even if the makeup of its body made it invulnerable to pain, even the elder dragon couldn't withstand countless stone shards exploding within its body.

Normally, no one would be stupid enough to challenge an elder dragon, and even if they were, such a fool would never be able to wound it. Even if they knocked it down or struck its little toe with a tree, they would never cause an elder dragon to feel pain.

Which meant elder dragons were unaccustomed to pain. Weak to it. This particular one was exceptionally so.

"H-hyou bwastaaaaaards!!!"

The dragon bellowed in pain and rage at the humiliation of being wounded by a lesser life-form.

Then it took a deep breath.

Without a doubt, it was preparing a specialty of all its kind: Dragon's Breath.

There was no time for Pauline, who had just finished firing a spell, or Reina, who was on the verge of finishing her next, to prepare any protection magic. Even if they had, any spell they could muster would be as tough as wet tissue against dragon fire.

The moment they saw the crimson flames blazing in the dragon's wide-open mouth, the two knew death was coming for them.

"Father, everyone...I'm so sorry..."

"All I wanted was to be with Alan and mother, and together we could..."

"Magic Shield!!!"

Dr. Clairia stepped into the fray. She had prepared her strongest protection spell and held it in waiting. Now, she channeled all her magical energy into an expansive shield. Even so, it wouldn't have held back an elder dragon's breath at full strength. Thankfully, this attack had been weak.

And of course it was weak. No matter how angry the dragon was, you wouldn't use a bomb to kill a mouse. There was also the fact that the dragon was unaware that amongst its opponents was an elf, a race far more skilled with magic than humans.

However, though the shield protected against the core of the breath attack—the flames and the heat—they still took the force head-on. The three of them were sent flying. Thankfully, they weren't blasted into the ruins as the two before had been but still soared an impressive distance. They plummeted to the ground, unlikely to rise again soon. The elder dragon, having already lost interest in them, ignored the three ladies and began to stalk toward Mile once more.

Oh no! I have to save her...

From her position collapsed on the ground, Mavis had seen everything. Now she tried her best to pull herself to her feet, but because she had struck her head, and her bones and tendons were injured, none of her limbs would cooperate.

I know, the Micross! If I just use the Micross...

Even with that solution in mind, her arms would not work the way she willed them to. Bit by bit they inched toward her side, but she had almost no sensation in her fingers. She couldn't find her pocket at all.

The elder dragon was already standing over Mile, reaching out its right arm.

No! I'm never gonna make it!

Just as Mavis plunged into despair, there was a sharp ringing in her ear. The sound gave her a strange sense of déjà vu...

Shiiiiiiing... Bang!!
"Gwaah!"

The elder dragon drew back its outstretched right arm in a panic, gripping its palm.

Mavis raised her eyes.

Could it be? If it was, then she would see, up in the sky...

And indeed, when Mavis looked up, she saw above her—

"Yahooo!"

—a girl about ten years old, shouting out. Beneath her, a familiar wyvern finished a drop attack and turned back to reascend.

"L-Lobreth!"

The singular reinforcement the region's lord had sent out had now arrived.

Lobreth, flapping high in the sky, once more began an easy descent, likely to use his breath attack once again. However, this was incredibly reckless.

"This pitiful excuse for a dragon dares to challenge me..."

Viewing the wyvern as a foe who could cause harm, the elder dragon took a defensive stance. Just as Lobreth approached at a shallow angle, opening his mouth wide to prepare another blast of breath...

Boom!

A fireball burst from the elder dragon's mouth.

This was nothing like the small flame it had fired toward Reina and the others; this was a *true* fireball, a sphere of searing death.

The high-velocity fireball smacked straight into Lobreth's left wing. He crashed into the trees with a scream from the girl upon his back. The curtain had fallen on Lobreth's performance just as quickly as it had risen.

However, those scant few moments weren't for naught. Within that narrow window Lobreth and the girl had granted them, Mavis finally managed to find her pocket, seized one of the capsules inside, and flipped the lid open.

"I'm counting on you, Micross!"

Just as Mile taught her, she said a word of prayer, "to increase the effectiveness," and gulped down everything inside. Every last drop.

"I can finish healing later. For now, I just need to focus my spirit, ignore the pain, and get this body moving! Let's goooooooooo!!!"

Mavis fought with all her might to control her body, harnessing her own powerful spirit. As she believed she couldn't use magic whatsoever, Mavis had no idea that what she was doing was, in fact, using healing magic.

As the pain vanished, and feeling and motion returned to her limbs, Mavis knew this didn't mean her wounds were truly healed. It meant she had stopped feeling the pain. Her spiritual power supported her bones and ligaments to the lowest necessary degree. However, that was enough for her.

She drew another capsule from her pocket, the third that day.

Mile's words ran through her head:

"Please only use one of these at a time. If you absolutely must, you can use just one more. However, if you do, please don't push your body too far. When you use these, your muscles and ligaments will compensate to a fair degree, but eventually they won't be able to keep up. If you overdo it, you'll end up with fractured bones and torn ligaments. Your whole body will fall apart.

"And whatever you do, avoid using three or more at all costs. You should use only one, at most two, in a time of crisis—and in those

*moments you need to exercise the utmost caution. Got that? If you
mess this up, you could end up dead!"*

However, Mile had also taught Mavis a special spell that
would smash through those rules, no matter how much Mile
tried to warn her. As Mavis swallowed the contents of the third
capsule, she uttered those words:

"To hell with that!"

Then, she took a fourth capsule, and a fifth, staring hard at
them. Mavis borrowed a decisive phrase Mile used now and then:

"If this isn't the time to use these, then when is?!"

And with that, she took the two last capsules.

Mavis's short sword, her main weapon, had been thrown who
knows where when the dragon sent her flying. All she had now
was the sword she'd brought from home, previously broken and
remade into a dagger by Mile. Smoothly, she drew her blade.

There was the faintest whisper... As the air around her began
to stir, Mavis grinned.

"Looks like this will be our first real battle together. I'm sorry
I've only used you for cooking up until now. This might be the first
and last time we ever fight as a pair, but please, give me your all!"

A tremor seemed to run through the dagger.

Scrtch...

"Hm?"

Scrtch, scrtch, scrtch...

Beads of light flowed from the dagger's blade. Then, upon it, a divine and brilliant, shining crest appeared.

"Is this your true form? Haha, never mind a dragon, I bet you could cut down a devil, or a god!"

It was the coating that had been applied to the blade to keep it from standing out and to dull the cutting edge. The nanomachines that clung to the dagger to maintain this coating had decided to remove it of their own volition.

Through many tearful days of misfortune, the nanomachines had heard Mile say those decisive words, too. Now they thought it to themselves:

IF NOW ISN'T THE TIME TO REMOVE THIS, THEN WHEN IS?!

If this knight was willing to put her life on the line for that girl, then they would aid her. This was the consensus of the nanomachines.

Mavis faced the elder dragon with this dagger in hand. She let out a battle cry.

For a short time, the elder dragon watched the trees, in case the wyvern had only pretended to fall and would try to send logs flying the elder dragon's way. But when it showed no sign of that, once again the dragon turned back toward the girls.

It was well aware the human who had attacked it with a sword before was heading its way. But even in top form, she had barely scratched its scales. She had lost her main weapon and now relied on a tiny, back-up blade. Plus, with her body still battered, there was no way she could do any harm.

Knowing this, the dragon allowed her to attack as she pleased.

It could easily have brushed her away with claw or tail, but allowing her to attack, allowing her to see she couldn't so much as wound it, would reinforce the futility and despair, as well as the fear of elder dragons that made them so legendary.

And so, the dragon struck a pose that let the girl know that while it knew she approached, it was completely ignoring her. It wouldn't even realize she had landed an attack. But then...

Stab.

"...Hm?"

The elder dragon froze.

"Hm? Huh? Wha...?" It was in such shock, its brain couldn't make the connection. It didn't even feel much pain.

Something had pierced its side, through tough scales and powerful hide, far deeper than the few inches the drill had managed. Only when it felt a red-hot, searing sensation coursing through its side did the dragon stop staring, dumbfounded.

"Grr-raaaaaaaaaaaaah!!"

With all her might, Mavis attempted to move the blade.

Learning from earlier failures, she hadn't tried to slice through. Instead she buried the blade deep into the dragon's flesh, so far that with another inch, the hilt would be engulfed.

From there, she had to move the blade again, but moving it from a dead stop would take tremendous strength; moving it after it had already pierced not only the tough hide and scales but the peritoneum and outer muscles, as well, was a high hurdle indeed.

If she only had to pull it straight out, it would have been comparatively easy. However, never minding the difference in their sizes meant targeting the dragon's heart was impossible, inflicting a large gash would cause the dragon far more damage, she thought. Whether her intuition was correct, she couldn't know.

"Nghhhhhhh..."

Mavis mustered all her strength to pull the blade sideways. Finally, with a crunch, she felt it move, just a little.

When she gave even more power, she felt it drag. Yes, it was definitely moving!

"Raaaaaaaaahh...!"

Rip.

From somewhere within Mavis's body, there was an unpleasant sound.

Rip, riiiiiip...

Snap!

"Gaah!"

Snap. Crackle. Rip. Pop!

"Waaaaaaaah!!"

"Graaaaaaaah!!"

Lagging behind a beat, the elder dragon, staring at the knife ripping through its belly, began to feel the pain. In a frenzy, it sent Mavis flying with its claw again. This time, she landed close to Reina and the others.

The other three had thankfully not lost consciousness, so they had managed to crawl behind a stone wall and heal each other with magic. When Mavis, seriously injured, was cast their way, they rushed out. All three concentrated their healing magic on her. Without paying sufficient attention to the elder dragon.

"Y-you measly humans..."

The elder dragon had managed to stop the bleeding from the wound in its gut with its own magic, but of course the wound itself didn't instantly recover. Outside of Mile, and Pauline, who had received her instruction, the only ones who could use such rapid healing magic were the Wonder Trio.

The dragon glared at the fallen Mavis, as well as the other three. It opened its mouth wide, drew in a great breath, and quickly, along with a bright flame...

Bam!

Ka-boom~!

It looked at the sky and fired the blast.

A rock had struck it in the face at the last second, forcing the elder dragon to change the direction it was facing.

"Who dares?!"

The dragon turned, froth and saliva dripping from its mouth in anger. Before it stood Mile, her armor, clothes, and hair in shambles. Just like the dragon, she trembled and seethed in anger, her stance imposing.

"Guess what?" she thrust her index finger forward and shouted at the dragon. "Now, you've made me *really* angry!"

Didn't I Say
to Make My Abilities
Average in the
——— Next Life?!

CHAPTER 34

A Battle of Magic

MILE WAS ANGRY. Her armor and clothing were in tatters. Her hair was a mess.

However, *this* wasn't the reason Mile was angry.

Her allies, her *friends*, had been hurt. They were very nearly killed. If she hadn't made it in time, they *would* have been killed. Her dearest companions, who fought their hardest and risked their own lives just to save her.

"Impossible... No human could recover so quickly from that much damage! You... just what *are* you?!" The elder dragon raged.

Mile stoically replied, "Me? I'm a completely normal, ordinary little girl and a C-rank hunter."

"Lies!! Show your true self!"

Bwoosh!

Shing!

"Wh..."

Knowing it would never learn the truth if it killed her, the dragon held back a bit, firing a small, non-explosive ball of flame Mile's way. Thanks to Mile's Lattice Power barrier, the flames were repelled as though they were nothing.

"I suppose I held back a bit too much... Well then, take this!"

Whoosh!

Shing!

"Th-then, this..."

Bwoosh!

Shing!

"I-Impossible! Very well, time to get serious..."

Bwoosh!

Shing!

"!..."

Bwoosh!

Shing!

Bwoosh!

Shing!

Bwoosh!

Shing!

"Wha..."

"Now, it's my turn," Mile declared. The elder dragon, stunned that its attack spells could be repelled so easily even when fired at full power, was silent. Mile let off an attack spell with a brief incantation. "Transmute the elements and channel phase energy. Phase energy beam, fire!"

Smeck!

With a very light sound, the spell shot into the elder dragon's left shoulder, right where arm and torso connected. Without any regard for the magical protection likely affixed to the dragon's body.

"Hm?"

The dragon's jaw half-dropped, as if it could not comprehend the current state of affairs. It was impossible to read a dragon's facial expressions, but anyone who looked at it now would agree that it appeared nothing more than flabbergasted.

And then, a beat later.

"Gaaaaaaaaah~~!!!"

The elder dragon's cry resounded through the trees.

How had Mile's magic, supposedly inferior to the dragon's, won in a fire fight? Why had her disposition shifted so drastically?

The reasons were two-fold.

For one, Mile was incredibly angry. Her immense rage had banished the fear, despair, and resignation roiling in her heart to a far corner of her mind.

But more importantly, Mile had realized something: The difference between her and the elder dragon's power wasn't so great after all.

Mile's abilities were perhaps half that of the strongest elder dragon in this world. However, this didn't mean they were half that of the elder dragon now standing before her. Judging by its behavior, this elder dragon was probably dead average between the most powerful elder dragons and those who were complete incompetents. In other words, at about half the strength of the strongest elder dragon. By that measure, Mile by no means possessed only half of *this* particular dragon's strength.

So, what if the strongest dragons were orders of magnitude higher in strength? What if this elder dragon wasn't in their league?

In that case, the difference between Mile's power and this dragon's wasn't so great, was it?

Plus, Mile had an advantage. She possessed all the knowledge and power of the imagination she carried from her past life.

She could conjure the image of a Type 94 naval gun or a 500-kilo bomb exploding, a beam weapon's power or the effects of a nuclear bomb. Although it was very unlikely the nanomachines would allow her to conjure an actual nuclear blast.

These were powerful, offensive images that this world could scarcely begin to imagine. They granted her overwhelming superiority.

Plus, with her knowledge of the principles of physical phenomena, she could conjure a relatively *concrete* image as well. And the nanomachines would automatically account for any deficiencies.

In other words, compared to someone who possessed the same amount of magical power, Mile was capable of far stronger, far more efficient spells. And the effect of that was:

In a battle between two swordsmen, even when there was a reasonable difference in raw power, the battle wasn't yet decided. The victory went to the one who could strike a blow to their opponent's vitals the quickest. Even the weaker of the two could still manage to pull a sudden victory in the end.

However, if one could completely deflect the other's magical attacks, while their own burst through the enemy's shield as though it were paper, then there would be no contest.

The victory was decided before the battle had even truly begun.

However, just then...

"What's all the racket up there? Shut up!"

"What's going on?"

Two more elder dragons crept out of the hole.

Of these two newcomers, one was a rank larger than the first dragon who had appeared. It looked from Pauline and Reina, who were trying desperately to heal Mavis, to Dr. Clairia, who was poised to cast another protection spell at any moment, to Mile and her tattered rags.

Then it issued a scathing rebuke to the first dragon.

"Wence! How many times do the elders have to tell you not to abuse lower life-forms? Er... or are *you* the one being abused here?"

Staring at the blood pouring from the wound on Wence's pierced shoulder, its eyes round, was the much-older elder dragon, Berdetice.

"Aha aha ha ha ha ha! That's so funny, Wence! An elder dragon, an *elder dragon* tormented by a human! Goodness, if you always made me laugh this hard, I would have never turned you down for a date!"

As Shelala, the daughter of the chief elder dragon, rolled on the ground laughing, Wence was so indignant he forgot the pain in his shoulder.

"Damn these humans, making me disgrace myself in front of Shelala... I won't forgive you!" Wence opened his mouth wide and let out another powerful breath attack.

"Wh—Stop that, you idiot!!"

Ignoring Berdetice's order to stop, Wence let out not a single fireball but a full-powered Dragon's Breath. Mile, standing before him, vanished, her body enveloped in flames.

"Wence, what have you done...?"

Seeing this senseless violence from Wence, who she had been ribbing and mocking, all the color drained from Shelala's face. No human would ever be able to tell, but to a dragon it was an unmistakable expression of distress, and an understandable one. It would be like a human girl seeing a kitten slaughtered right before her eyes.

"You've violated the 'Lesser Life-forms Protection Act'! A decree from our elders!"

Just as Berdetice began to speak, the young elder dragon, Wence, finally ceased his attack.

Standing there before their eyes was Mile, completely unharmed.

"Impossible..."

"What?"

"Huh???"

Wence stood there in disbelief. Berdetice and Shelala's eyes were wide with shock.

Mile, however, was panicking. Just when she thought she could turn this battle around, one dragon became three. Her chances of victory were slim. Knowing she had no choice but to better her odds, she decided to fire an attack spell. Her aim: the first dragon to appear, the one who held so much malice for her and her friends. The other two seemed more diplomatic.

Judging by the state of things, it would be bad to kill him. The fighting strength of the belligerent dragon was weak, and she should probably try to work out a way to talk with the biggest dragon. If that was impossible, the third dragon was small, at least. With one of each size, depending on the circumstances, she might be able to eke out a victory.

So Mile thought as she fired a spell at Wence.

"Phaser, fire!"

The moment Mile attacked, the dragon known as Berdetice stepped out from behind Wence and put up a protection spell.

Shunk!

"Gaaaaaaah!"

Wence cried out as this time, the beam struck deep into his right arm. Berdetice, meanwhile, panicked, seeing how the spell had gone right through his full power protective shield.

"Shelala, get behind me! Calm down, Wence! We have to fight together!"

Berdetice was truly flustered. He was facing the impossible: a being who could harm an elder dragon.

Even though the chances were one in a million, he couldn't allow harm to come to Shelala. Wounds could be mended with magic, but the idea of Shelala being hurt at all was unpleasant. He recoiled at the thought of what the chief and the elders, who were ever so fond of Shelala, would do to him if they found out he had exposed her to harm or let her know pain.

Knowing that Berdetice was on his side, Wence collected himself. The wound stung badly, but he knew he could count on Shelala and her special healing magic to put him back together once they were through. Now, above all else, their greatest priority was to remove this dangerous, uncertain element.

"Breath, release!"

At Berdetice's signal, the three elder dragons fired their breath attacks toward Mile.

What of the "Inferior Life-forms Protection Act" Berdetice had mentioned?

That only applied to helpless creatures—a sort of warrior's hypocrisy. When it came to situations of true danger, however, such rules were easily ignored.

No matter how much she reinforced it, Mile's protection spell wasn't impressive enough to completely shield her from a breath attack from *three* elder dragons. With a sharp *ka-shing!*, the lattice power barrier shattered easily, the course of the attack averted only slightly. Mile's left arm was engulfed.

"Ngah!!"

Putting the searing pain aside, she forewent healing magic to fire another attack spell. "Phaser, fiiiiiiire!!!"

Shing!

However, with the strength of the dragons combined, their shield easily reflected Mile's counterattack. And then, the dragons fired a combined breath attack once again.

Mile, her face contorted in pain, immediately put up another full-strength barrier. While it shattered again, it at least sufficiently repelled most of the breath's power. The remainder of it still struck, however, and Mile was once again blown backward, sent flying into the stone walls of the ruins.

"Guh-haah!!"

Once more, Mile collapsed to the ground.

I can't win.

Of course, I can't. There's no way I could win against three *elder dragons.*

But that's not a reason to give up! My life and the lives of everyone else. That's what's on the line.

Mile clenched her teeth hard.

Okay then. It's time to really do this. There's three of them, so I need to summon up the strength of three, don't I?

There's Kurihara Misato, the girl who died at eighteen.

There's Adele von Ascham, the young noble girl, whose consciousness was combined with mine at ten.

And then, there's the girl I am now: Mile of the Crimson Vow, the C-rank hunter who fights alongside her friends, who's achieved all I dreamed of in my past life.

All three of my lives, all three of their dreams. Their hopes and their feelings. If the enemies are three-fold, then I have to summon three-fold strength as well, don't I?

And so, once more, Mile stood, staring the three dragons down all the while.

"Oho, still standing, are you? You should know there's no way you can beat us. If you humbly admit defeat, and tell us everything, we'll spare your friends' lives and yours," said the elder dragon, Berdetice.

To which, Mile replied, "You're the ones who have no chance of winning. If you humbly admit defeat, and tell me everything, I'll spare your friends' lives and yours..."

"Hm...?"

"Bwa ha ha, what a funny little one! Humans are such precious things."

Ignoring the elder dragons' responses, Mile incanted her spell:

"Nanomachines!"

At the loudly shouted word, there was crackling all around, as though the air was freezing over.

"NANOMACHINES! JE VOUS COMMANDE..." So the elder dragons wouldn't understand her spell, Mile commanded the nanomachines in a language found in her past life. Even if the nanomachines were unable to understand Terran languages, as long as they received her thought pulse, there would be no miscommunication. Plus, she got the feeling God had trained them in at least that much, on her behalf.

The next command she gave in Japanese.

"*Kurihara Misato, Adele von Ascham, soshite Mile ga meizuru. Waga meirei wo, saiyuusen de judaku seyo...*"

("Kurihara Misato, Adele von Ascham, and Mile command you. Accept our commands above all others...")

"No matter how many times you try, it's useless. There's no way you can pass through a shield formed by three elder drag—"

Ka-shnk, boom!

"Wh..."

The three elder dragons were dumbstruck as their protective shield was shattered in a single hit.

"N-no way... That's impossible! The shield we three elder dragons have formed was shattered by some puny human's Fire Lance...?"

Hearing this, Mile grinned. Yes, the time had come for her to say one of the lines she had hoped to speak at least once in her lifetime. She couldn't hold back her joy.

"That wasn't even my amazing Fire Lance. That was only a little Fire Ball..."

At Mile's words, the dragons' eyes widened in fear. Their jaws went slack.

However, that *had* been a Fire Lance fired at full power. It was important to bluff a little now and then in battle, after all.

Why was it that Mile's magical power had suddenly increased so immensely?

It was just as the nanomachines had explained in their very

first conversation, when the first water spell Mile had used after her awakening had gone so explosively:

YOU ISSUED A DIRECT COMMAND TO WE NANOMACHINES, SO THE EFFECTIVENESS OF THE SPELL WAS INCREASED 3.27 TIMES OVER.

Given that, what would happen if Mile, with her level five authorization, issued an even more precise, clearer command than before?

Indeed, the result would be what you just saw.

"I-Impossible... This cannot be... W-we must attack at full power!"

Boom!

The three swells of breath were deflected and dispersed just before they struck Mile.

"H-how, how could this..."

"Thunder Bolt!"

Ka-boom!

A bolt of lightning struck Wence. With a great tremor, he fell to the ground, his eyes wide.

"L-Lightning? Her magic can control nature!"

Even an elder dragon wouldn't understand the concept of electricity, so lightning magic was likely beyond them.

"Feel like surrendering yet? Oh, by the by, this magic can strike from above, so there's no use hiding behind one another. If you don't surrender now, then that one back there will be n..."

"Roooooooooooooaaaawwwrrr!!"

Berdetice let out a great roar in Mile's direction. He absolutely couldn't allow an attack to come Shelala's way! The human could block any of their magical attacks, and they couldn't block hers. And if the magic came from above, he couldn't act as Shelala's shield.

What could he do? The answer was simple.

If magic was no use, then he had to best her with a physical attack. There was nothing else to do. He charged her.

There wasn't a creature alive who could stand up to an elder dragon in physical combat. He began to pick up momentum now, so that, even if he should be bested by the enemy's attack magic, his body would still fall upon her and crush her.

This is it! Berdetice thought, but he was puzzled and a bit unsettled that the human showed no signs of moving.

Well, I'm sure she's stunned senseless by the awe of an elder dragon coming her way! There couldn't be any other reason.

Mile didn't move, not even at the end. And just like that, Berdetice stomped upon her.

"Gaaaaaaaah!!!"

Berdetice suddenly found his right foot, which should have flattened Mile into the dirt, impaled by a silver sword.

Mile, after all, was skilled not only at magical combat but in close-range combat as well.

Berdetice lifted his foot in a panic, revealing Mile beneath it, standing unharmed. All the injuries she had taken were now completely healed. Her hair was back in order, as well. Unfortunately, however, her armor and clothing were still full of holes.

"Wh-why?! Why aren't you smashed to pieces?!"

"Only a peon or a fool would blab the secrets of their techniques to the enemy, yes? Are you such a fool?"

"Wh-what...?"

Until the current battle, Mile had been convinced that her own body possessed half of an elder dragon's sturdiness. However, owing to her previously shattered bones, she now knew that wasn't the case.

If she thought about it, this made sense. Her bones, muscles, and tendons were nowhere near the size of an elder dragon's, so she couldn't possibly have half their strength or power. Not unless she had an orichalcum skeleton or woven-carbon nanotube muscles.

Even for a (so-called) God, it was probably impossible to make something human-sized, out of the normal human materials, that was stronger than a human. At the very least, impossible to do while still calling such a creation "human."

So how had Mile prevailed?

It was her body-strengthening magic.

Compared to Mavis, Mile's body and basic abilities were in a league of their own. She could withstand a fair bit of strengthening magic. Plus, Mile had gathered a number of nanomachines within her body. With this, she could administer healing magic to herself and petition the nanomachines directly.

In other words, even without drinking the microsoup, she could conjure the same effect. Times several hundreds, or thousands.

Naturally, this was still not enough for her to be able to flip an elder dragon or anything, but as long as she could withstand the weight, then with the barrier applied to her own skin and her sturdy strengthening magic, she could manage *something*.

Or rather, she had.

"Since you don't appear interested in surrendering, I'll just have to strike that one back there with my special magic. The magic that can lop off the head of any creature in an instant. My 'headhunting magic'..."

"St-stooooooooooooop!! St-stop it, pleeeeeease!!!"

Thud!

As Berdetice pled desperately, there was a great rumbling. Everyone turned to see the elder dragon known as Shelala—who could be assumed to be a girl, from the way the conversation had been going—behind Berdetice, faceup on the ground, her arms and legs splayed.

Until now, Dr. Clairia had been standing in steadfast concentration, ready to raise a shielding spell for Reina and the others, should the need arise. Now though, she relaxed her shoulders and said, "*That's* an elder dragon's pose of ultimate surrender."

Wence was incapacitated, Shelala had surrendered, and Berdetice couldn't continue to fight. Shelala's safety mattered above all else. Even Berdetice himself had lost the will to fight. He hadn't been fighting because he wanted to, after all. If they could resolve this by talking, there was no reason to go beyond that.

And now Shelala, who he was sworn to protect, had already surrendered. Berdetice had no choice but to lower his head, to signal, "Please, let us talk this over." He couldn't allow himself to be overwhelmed by anger at these unbelievable circumstances or his pride as an elder dragon.

And so, limply, Berdetice uttered,

"We surrender..."

Didn't I Say
to Make My Abilities
Average in the
Next Life?!

CHAPTER 35 |

The Ruins

AFTER EVERYONE HAD CAUGHT THEIR BREATH, they stepped away from the beastmen. The 5-on-3 tribune between the three elder dragons and the Crimson Vow Plus One began. They conversed near the great hole in the ground. The elder dragons wouldn't have fit inside any structure, so they had no choice but to hold it out in the open.

Berdetice, who sat on the ground facing the humans, was riled up during the fight, but he had calmed down now. This was quite a boon.

Wence, who, perhaps owing to his youth, was rash and hot-blooded, was quiet now, which was nothing short of astounding.

Shelala, meanwhile, was very collected. She seemed incredibly bold for someone who had surrendered the moment she thought danger might befall her.

"First off, I would like to confirm something," Mile said. "You elder dragons were undoubtedly the ones to give the beastfolk the order to operate at this site, yes? Also, you three aren't operating independently but in conjunction with your whole clan?"

"That's correct," Berdetice answered Mile's question plainly. Or, at least truthfully. Perhaps he was a creature of integrity, or the topic was of little importance, or else he simply thought it was a nonissue if any humans knew.

Truthfully, he was merely praying he wouldn't later regret not keeping his mouth shut.

"What exactly is your aim?"

Whether this was a conversation or an interrogation, Mile served as the Crimson Vow's representative. There was no one else who would ask the right questions.

Dr. Clairia had also prepared some questions of her own, should the need arise, but for now she remained a spectator, simply watching Mile work.

The representative for the elder dragons was Berdetice, who seemed to be the oldest. The other two didn't seem to have any interest in participating in the conversation.

"We are conducting an exploratory excavation." Berdetice answered, but the chances of him not lying and not telling the truth were equally probable. In cases like this, the questioner had to rely on their knowledge, intuition, and strength.

"What are you searching for?"

His answer was a bit delayed. In fact, it wasn't much of an answer at all. **"...Ruins."**

Excavating ruins in search of... more ruins.

This didn't seem to be a lie, but it was an evasive answer. And one Mile wasn't willing to accept and leave it at that.

"What are you searching for? Treasure? Intelligence? Some sort of tool or a demon king? An evil spirit, a monster, a weapon, some magical item, an ancient machine?"

Berdetice was silent. Clearly, they had come to a point he didn't wish to talk about.

"If you aren't going to talk about this, then we can't have much of a conversation. How do you think the humans are going to take those beastmen—moreover, the beastmen who are going to be associated with you elder dragons as a whole—invading human lands to perform some kind of suspicious operation? If this is deemed an act of aggression, a large-scale war is going to break out. A war between humans, elder dragons, and beastpeople is sure to have tremendous casualties on all sides."

"We have no such intention!"

"Whether you do or don't, that is the situation you are threatening to bring about. Suppose one day, some humans, elves, and dwarves decide to band together and invade the elder dragons' territory unannounced. Then they start some suspicious construction work. Elder dragons who go to investigate it are attacked, and then one after another they go missing. If a human were to say to the dragons, 'Oh, we don't have bad intentions,' would the dragons *really* allow them to continue undisturbed?

"If that's the case, then you would see *a lot* of humans going about under that pretense. They would just assume they could do whatever they want within your territory. Do you want to just go ahead and write up a contract saying that now?"

"Wh-what foolishness is this?"

"Are you not doing the exact same thing?"

Berdetice was silent.

"Your response may mean the difference between an all-out war and avoiding conflict entirely. Please think carefully before you answer."

After what felt like an eternity, Berdetice finally opened his mouth. **"...A 'lost civilization.'"**

"Hm?"

"It is said that in this world, in the distant past, there was a land that was home to a highly advanced civilization. It is nothing more than a legend... Well, it was *thought* to be nothing more than a legend, but now..."

"But now?"

"We believe we have discovered proof of their existence."

"Whaaaaaaaaaaaaaaaaat?!?!" Dr. Clairia shouted from the sidelines. "D-d-don't tell me you've uncovered proof of the existence of the 'Antiquated Land'?!"

"D-did you know about this, Clare?" Mile had reflexively tried to make a joke, but it only made the scholar angry.

"Don't start giving me weird nicknames!" Dr. Clairia snapped. She took a breath and cleared her throat.

"The Antiquated Land," she explained, "was a legendary kingdom that thrived in the far distant past. While the rest of humanity sat around at home, these people observed the world. It's said they plunged to the bottom of the sea and flew through the sky. That they even soared beyond the sky itself to touch the stars. They never knew famine nor war. It was the sort of divine land even the gods themselves might deem fit to dwell in.

"Because the seasons turn so quickly amongst humans, knowledge of these people has been all but lost. Among the longer-lived species, though, like elves and elder dragons, and among spirits and the like, their legend lives on."

When Dr. Clairia said "flew through the sky," Reina's face twitched. Mile, however...

"Y-you mean spirits really exist?! Like f-faeries?" As usual, she had latched onto the least relevant part.

The scholar was, understandably, livid. "That has nothing to do with the conversation!! Anyway, this is a huge discovery, if it's true! Dragons, what kind of proof did you find?! Where did you find it?! How?!"

Watching Clairia babble and foam at the mouth, the elder dragon Berdetice became troubled.

"I-I don't know. None of us are scholars by trade. Elder dragonfolk can't travel all over the place investigating, so we enlist demons and beastfolk to conduct excavations in our stead. Then we go to the site to confirm what they've found. We're nothing more than the liaison. They even got children involved this time... Er, never mind!"

Seeing Shelala glare at him, Berdetice swiftly changed the topic.

"Anyway, we received a missive from the beastfolk they had discovered something, and so we three—myself, my apprentice,

Wence, and Shelala, who cajoled the chief and the elders into letting her come along—came to inspect their findings. That's it. Furthermore, the results of our finding are that the artifact here was a 'miss.'"

"Dragon*folk*"? Mile cocked her head at the unfamiliar phrasing. As she thought about it, though, it began to make since. Humans didn't think of themselves as some sort of animal when speaking of their own race, so it wasn't all that strange that dragons referred to themselves as "people" as well.

Before she could spiral into more frivolous pondering, Mile snapped back to reality.

"A miss?" she asked.

"Indeed. It is nothing more than an artifact made sometime after the 'Lost Epoch,' by a people who deified said-epoch's people. There are some fantastic, incomprehensible drawings that were discovered on the walls of what might be a great temple, but they don't appear to mean anything.

"We have no more use for this place. We will ask the beast-folk to withdraw. Then they will no longer trouble you!"

Berdetice attempted to wrap up the conversation there, but this couldn't end quite so simply.

"You're all finished, you say? So you're just going to go start up somewhere else, then? You're going to secretly invade some other place and start capturing its people?" demanded Mile.

"..."

"And you have not only beastpeople but also demons in your employ?"

Berdetice, who suddenly realized he had let unnecessary information slip, clammed up.

"And for what purpose exactly are you searching for this 'lost civilization'? Just what do you intend to do?"

"I don't know! Even if I did, I couldn't just tell you all about it!"

That much was probably true. Prisoners of war often said nothing, and what he had told them so far was probably all he deemed safe to tell them in order to avoid a war. Plus, there was the possibility he truly *didn't* have all the answers. It wasn't a stretch to think an underling wouldn't have been given the full story.

From the elder dragon's appearance and his manners, one could mistake him for a dragon of importance. Judging by their conversation, though, he was clearly no one special, at least as far as elder dragons went. He was a lowly errand boy, still green behind the ears. The less said about *his* apprentice, and the dragon heiress who had merely tagged along out of curiosity, the better.

Getting more information out of them was futile. Capturing and turning over elder dragons to the local lord was probably equally futile. Becoming an enemy of a dragon clan was still possible and could prove disastrous.

In all things, knowing when something was on the brink of becoming something else was far more crucial—and far more difficult—than the initial timing of when those things began. Mile understood this from the news, historical reports, and war records she had absorbed during her life on Earth. As they stood now, as mere C-rank hunters, their duty wasn't to go about capturing elder dragons and starting wars between different races.

Those things were for important folks of the land to decide and for people of equivalent standing—or who had been suitably rewarded—to undertake. At the very least, it wasn't a task for four rookie hunters who had been paid a few dozen gold pieces.

"Understood. Well, please show us these ruins, and then we'll depart," Mile said. "If you really have no more business in this place, then please desert it quickly. If you can, try and get out of here before the king's soldiers arrive and this turns into a big mess.

"We'll tell this region's lord just enough to avoid problems, but that information *is* going to end up going to the palace. They'll be keeping this in mind as a reference for future encounters. They'll probably be on guard, should they come across you. Are you fine with that?"

After pondering for a short while, Berdetice nodded. **"Please do so, then."**

Mile looked left and right. Reina, Mavis, Pauline, and Dr. Clairia nodded as well.

Dr. Clairia had come to this conclusion as an investigator of a lord, as a researcher, and as an elf. The decision to agree came naturally.

"Miss Shelala, will you show us the way?"

"Oh, me?"

Shelala seemed shocked to be called upon, but for Mile, she was the obvious choice. Going underground before the eyes of three elder dragons, who might turn on them at any moment was a bad choice—almost as bad as going alone with someone as powerful as Berdetice. If they could bring the weakest dragon along as a hostage—er, an effective guide—then that was the best option.

Still, Mile silently cast a barrier over them. Just in case.

"Now then, shall we?"

With the dragon girl (though you wouldn't be able to tell just from looks) Shelala as their guide, the group descended into the great hole. After passing through some rubble and unsettled earth that was probably displaced when the hole first opened up, they came to an open space. From there, they entered an area that seemed like a great hall. This was most likely the "temple" Berdetice had mentioned.

Because Shelala was so large, she couldn't enter the hall itself. If they forced her, the temple would probably collapse upon them all.

To avoid this, Shelala stuck her neck through the opening. Even before they'd come above ground some time ago, it seemed the three dragons had only stuck their heads in to see.

"Now then, Miss Shelala, what I've attached to your neck is a very thin but incredibly strong cord. If you move your neck too quickly, then..."

Mile drew a line across her throat.

"Ee-eeeeeeeeeek!" Though Shelala could be thought of as rather bold, once her life was at stake she was a coward.

With that threat in place to ensure the dragon wouldn't run, Mile and the others entered the hall.

"Light!"

With Mile's spell, light spread throughout the space.

"Th-this place is…"

As the light grew, the hall came into view. It wasn't especially spacious. There was no altar nor any religious artifacts to be found. A completely empty space surrounded them.

However, they could soon see why Berdetice had called this place a "temple."

The walls. *All* the walls of this dome-like room were covered in murals.

These murals hadn't been made with brush and paint. They were magnificent tile-work masterpieces, formed from a myriad of colored stones and painstaking thought as to how to bring them together. They were the products of labor that took unthinkable amounts of time and effort.

At closer inspection, they discovered they weren't tiles, per se, as every stone wasn't flat. In any case, stones in a great variety of colors joined together to create the images upon the stone walls.

Given that none of these stones had faded or fallen over who knew how many years, whoever constructed the murals must not have merely affixed them. They had devised some technique to drive the stones into the wall itself. This wasn't surprising; anyone who would spend this much time on something like this wasn't likely to cut corners.

Reina, Mavis, Pauline, and Dr. Clairia were all stunned at these impressive works of craftsmanship. Mile, however, standing stock-still with her mouth half-open, wasn't thinking about the impressive amount of labor involved.

"Wh-what is this…?"

To the other people, this is probably how the scene would have looked: strange vegetation growing in clumps, fish and jellyfish. Was this the bottom of the sea, then?

Humans, elves, dwarves, beastpeople, and demons all existing in harmony—an image of an ideal future. Beside them was a draconic form very much like an elder dragon, as well.

There were various other scenes in the mural. Other life forms and unidentifiable things, all crafted from stones in countless hues.

"A fantasy..." said Mavis.

"This is the first time I've seen anything like this..." said Reina.

"It would be nice if the world really could achieve a peace like this..." added Pauline.

The three murmured as they stared at the walls. Dr. Clairia, however, was silent, a troubled look upon her face.

As for Mile...

"Wh-what is going on here?"

The mural was vastly different to Mile's knowing eyes: rows of crowded skyscrapers, spaceships in ascension. Something like flying cars passing one another in the air. Humans dressed in researchers' garb. Members of other races, ranging from infancy to childhood.

And, curled up beside them, a small dragon, looking like nothing so much as a pet dog.

Somehow, Mile understood.

These pieces weren't someone's wild imagination, cobbled together in some flight of fancy.

These were images someone had known they absolutely had

to leave for future generations. They had devoted immense time and effort, perhaps even the rest of their lives, to crafting them in a way that would last.

If you wanted information to survive across centuries, the natural thing to do was draw a picture. That way, your idea would get across perfectly. That is probably why they put so much effort into constructing these murals.

For how many seasons did they hope these images would stand the test of time?

Who did they hope would see them?

That was when Mile remembered.

Back within that void, the so-called "God" had said to her:

"In truth, this world has collapsed a number of times, leaving only a scant number of survivors with meager skills. To offer relief measures, and as to conduct an experiment, we decided to interfere on a scale beyond what we would normally attempt."

That interference was, of course, Mile's old friends, the nanomachines.

Just like the professor, Mile stood wordless and still.

"Well, that'll be all for us. Please vacate these premises quickly. If you want to avoid conflict with humans, anyway..."

"Wait!"

As promised, once they finished investigating the ruins, the humans prepared to leave, but Berdetice stopped them.

"It is unfair that we were the only ones who had to give up any information. We will need to report to our superiors, too. I demand you provide us with information as well!"

What a bother, Mile thought, but what the dragon said was fair. They likely would have to make some report, so coming back with nothing wouldn't cut it. It was hard to be underlings and middlemen.

Besides, the Crimson Vow had only done precisely what any humans would do, so they had nothing to hide. Thinking about it that way, it would be rude to decline.

"What do you wish to know?" asked Mile.

Berdetice hoisted one enormous finger and thrust it Mile's way.

"You! Reveal your true nature!"

"Huh...?"

Everyone stared at Mile. Dr. Clairia seemed particularly invested.

It couldn't be helped. So Mile decided to answer his question frankly.

"My true nature? Very well, I'll tell you. My true nature is..."

Reina, Mavis, and Pauline held their breath.

"Once upon a time, I was the only daughter of a viscount. Another time, I was a C-rank hunter. However, my true form is..."

Dr. Clairia gulped.

"Mile, a completely ordinary, commonplace, average girl!"

"THAT'S A LIIIIIIEEEE!!!!!!"

Everyone present shouted in chorus.

"**Cease with your lies! You expect me to believe you are a mere human?!**" Berdetice demanded.

"You can doubt me, but my pedigree on both my mother and father's sides goes back for generations as part of a noble line. And I don't think there's been any blood of other races mixed with my ancestry in at least ten generations."

"**Wh-what...?**" Berdetice was stunned at the reply. "**I-I mean, I don't smell anything but human on you... Still, you shouldn't be so...**"

In a panic, Mile started sniffing herself. She *did* smell pretty sweaty, but she couldn't help that! She couldn't!!!

"**Well then, why are you so strong?! How can you stand up to an elder dragon?!**"

Mile whipped a finger out and answered proudly, "Because there are tremors in my soul and a fire in my heart!"

"**Hm? A-are you sure you're really a pure-blooded human? You truly are something else!**"

Mile grinned at this dire assertion, and replied, "Ah, yes, well I mean, I *was* born in a different country, so..."

Reina groaned. "He said you were *something* else, not from *somewhere* else!!"

Mile relaxed. Ah, some things would never change.

Leaving the three stunned dragons behind them, the Crimson Vow and Dr. Clairia departed from the site.

Ka-thud, ka-thud.

Something appeared from behind the trees.

"L-Lobreth!!!!" *We completely forgot about them...*

It was an awfully cruel thing to forget the ones who had saved their hides, if only briefly.

The girl who clung to Lobreth's neck jumped nimbly down, ran up to the group, opened her mouth, and said, "Arf arf!"

"E-Elsiiiiiiiiiiiiiiiiiiiieeeee?!?!"

"Oh, my name is Chelsea. I'm Lobreth's rider. We were dispatched here as your reinforcement!"

"Huuuuuuuuuh?!?!"

According to the young girl's story—which she told gladly as they healed the large wound on Lobreth's left wing—things hadn't gone as planned for Old Man Mage (whose name they had already forgotten).

He had said to the lord, "I wish to live in the King's capital," but that wouldn't have profited the lord in the slightest, so the lord had refused.

It made sense. The ones who had been harmed were the soldiers and citizens of that territory. If he let the mage go to the capital, and he managed to wheedle his way into the palace through his old connections or something, the lord and his lands would benefit in no way, shape, or form. All the damages they had received would total out to a net loss.

By comparison, keeping a wyvern that listened to human commands and the mage who had devised those commands with them, and having them work for the good of the territory, was a huge boon.

Besides, all that happened in the territory was within the lord's jurisdiction. He was under no obligation to turn a known criminal to the palace. Here, his word was law, and he could order whatever punishment he saw fit, including making the old man teach the secrets of controlling the wyvern to others. For free.

At first, when compelled to reveal the secrets behind wyvern training, the mage, who was under house arrest, had just prattled away. But after his continued obstinance, the word "torture" began to be bandied about, and he soon became far more helpful. Which was to say, he had befriended Lobreth "by chance," and there was no training method.

The indignant lord confiscated any pay the mage might receive and distributed it to the villagers and soldiers who had been harmed by the wyvern instead.

It came to pass that Lobreth and his singular war potential were drafted into the lord's military, and soon a rider needed to be selected. Lobreth, however, loathed to let any soldier ride upon his back. Not to mention that if a full-grown man clad in armor with weapons mounted him, the magical energy needed for Lobreth to stay aloft would increase, leading to his range and combat abilities dropping drastically. Thankfully, there wasn't a soldier around who was raring to ride the wyvern.

Finally, the lord asked the mage's opinion. From among all the young girls with no family—someone who was light of body, needed no armor, wouldn't disobey orders, and was expendable— one who had the aptitude was selected.

The young girl now stood before them, a girl who had previously known nothing but poverty and hunger in the slums.

"I never had a name. People just called me things like 'Dirt' and 'Trash', but Sir Byrnclift gave me a wonderful name: Chelsea! Since then, the two of us and Lobreth have lived a wonderful life together. Sir Byrnclift taught me how to fly. I'm never hungry, and I get a real bed to sleep in. Life with Lobreth and Sir Byrnclift is truly a dream come true." The girl sounded positively blissful as she told her tale.

What was most surprising was she had an accurate grasp of the mage's circumstances. Perhaps he had told her himself, perhaps she had heard it elsewhere, or perhaps she had caught snatches of gossip and pieced the story together. At any rate, she had exceptional faculties of reasoning for a ten-year-old girl from the slums.

Even though she knew the mage wasn't a man of good reputation, her gratitude to him as her benefactor, and the obligation she felt towards him, were great indeed. Even though she knew she was being used as a tool.

"For some reason, though, he always makes me greet and reply to him with 'Arf arf!'... Why is that? He's treating me like a dog, even lower than a servant, isn't he? Even so, Sir Byrnclift has shown me a lot of affection."

"Aha ha ha ha ha ha..."

Weak, empty laughter spilled forth from the Crimson Vow.

The Crimson Vow were a bit surprised. The suspicion that the lord was not such a bad person after all began to cross their minds. Well, whether it was correct to call that a "suspicion" was uncertain.

At the very least, the reinforcement he had sent out wasn't just an observer, but truly his greatest trump card, dispatched just in time. And he had distributed the mage's wages to the victims of the wyvern attacks, along with other sorts of things a noble wouldn't normally do. The mage, who had only been sentenced to work instead of punishment, didn't deserve wages in the first place, so perhaps it had been a decision made with some regard for the victims after all.

Plus, it seemed he had still given the mage and Chelsea enough provisions to live comfortably, even though there was probably not a person around who would complain if a criminal and an orphan from the slums were treated as the lowest of the low.

Reina was the first to say it: "Could it be this lord is actually a pretty decent guy?"

"He did pay us pretty well last time..." Naturally, Pauline's criteria for a "good person" was a little different from everyone else's.

Well, no matter what, he *had* provided for everyone's happiness in one way or another. That was a splendid thing.

While they talked, Lobreth's injuries were, eventually, completely healed. This was of little surprise, as he had three talented mages—Mile, Pauline, and Dr. Clairia—to heal him. With this much power on hand, they could probably bring someone back to life from even decapitation. If they weren't brain-dead, that is.

"Oh, Dr. Clairia, why don't you mount up with Chelsea and ride back to the capital ahead of us?" Mile suggested. "It would be better to get a report back to them before any soldiers or messengers are sent out from the capital, wouldn't it? In which case, it would be best to get the information to the guild or the lord first."

"Whuh? Huhhh?" Clairia appeared unsettled by Mile's proposal. She had hoped to remain by Mile's side and uncover her secrets.

But she would admit she really wanted to fly through the sky! She might never get another chance like this in her entire life!

On the *other* hand, flying also sounded super scary!

That said, she had accepted a job, and she had a duty to deliver the information as quickly as possible. The lord was probably already preparing his soldiers, without waiting for word from the palace.

A whirlpool of feelings spun around her head. It was impossible to collect her thoughts.

"B-but, won't Lobreth hate that...?" Somehow, this was the only reply Dr. Clairia could muster.

"Lobreth, you'll be fine, right? You'd be happy to let her ride, wouldn't you?" Mile said with a grin.

Lobreth's head bobbed up and down, like a broken toy.

After uncertainly flapping his healed wing a number of times, Lobreth finally accepted that it was better. He calmed down, then took off, with Chelsea and Dr. Clairia upon his back.

Before they departed, the scholar conferred with the others to decide who should receive what information.

Of course, the three elder dragons, standing silently nearby, heard this, so they should have understood the humans intended to tell their employer the truth, but with some intentional omissions, so as to lower the possibility of inciting a conflict.

There was still a chance that, as elder dragons continued to investigate ruins with beastfolk and demons as their proxies, someday, somewhere, a conflict would arise with them and humans, dwarves, or elves. However, that would be a matter for whoever was involved at that time. The Crimson Vow were by no means obligated to be part of every quarrel everywhere. They hadn't signed any such contract, after all.

That was something some other hunter or hero might take on. Probably for a nice sum of coins or the hand of a princess.

Without being hired to do so, any more needless meddling or confiscation would be unforgivable.

"Well then, it's time for us to really get going. The Crimson Vow's job is complete! Time to return to the capital!"

"Yeah!!!"

Now that Dr. Clairia wasn't around, the reply to Reina's decree was perfectly unanimous. Thus the Crimson Vow set out for the capital, leaving behind the three elder dragons, who watched silently as the girls walked away.

"Berdetice..." Shelala said softly.

"What?" Berdetice replied.

"Are you sure we can't follow them?"

"Bwha?! Wh-what are you saying?!"

"I know we can't, I was just asking."

"...I see."

However, Berdetice got the feeling he knew why Shelala was asking that. It was because, by some small degree, he felt the same way. Somehow he knew that if they traveled with those girls, their days would never be boring again, at least not as long as they were together.

Indeed, though their lifespans were nothing compared to the nanomachines, elder dragons lived for quite a long time and so were rather prone to boredom.

Didn't I Say
to Make My Abilities
Average in the
Next Life?!

Worries

"NOW OUR REPORT to the guild is going to be exactly as we discussed. Dr. Clairia already made a report to the lord, so there's probably no need for us to do another one. Us making a report to the guild is really just for the sake of appearances. The guild master was probably present when she made her report, after all," Reina mused as they walked. The others nodded in agreement.

The report to be given to the lord, as established during their prior discussion with Dr. Clairia (while the three elder dragons listened; Chelsea having excused herself to check on Lobreth's condition), was as followed:

The beastpeople were excavating ruins on the order of the elder dragons. This was being done for the sake of the elder dragons' research. The beastfolk were operating out of a sense of obligation to the dragons and working for scant pay, so they had no intention of actually invading the territory.

The ruins consisted of nothing but a number of long-abandoned stone buildings, some with fantastic murals inside. As the site was deemed a "miss" by the elder dragons, the beastfolk were already making preparations to withdraw. Even if soldiers headed to the site now, they would likely find no one there.

At first, the hired hunters were discovered by the beastmen and a fight erupted, which was interrupted by the sudden appearance of the elder dragons. They then returned all the equipment previously taken from the investigation team.

At the very least, nothing in the report was untrue.

They merely neglected to mention that the skirmish between their party and the beastmen and dragons had been an all-out battle.

Even if they told the truth, all it would do was stir up fear and suspicion among humans. In any case, there wasn't a soul who would believe that four young girls had gone toe-to-toe with dozens of beastmen and three elder dragons—and *won*.

If they handled this poorly, there was a chance they would be labeled liars, accused of not going to the site at all and making up tall tales. They might not get paid, if that happened. It wouldn't matter what endorsement Dr. Clairia gave, either. The professor herself might be denied pay and called a liar as well, which would be a huge blow to her reputation.

And if someone *did* believe their full report, it would undoubtedly open up a whole new can of worms.

Four young girls who could win against scores of beastmen and three elder dragons without backup?

They would be hounded. By the people here and everywhere else.

Thankfully, Chelsea hadn't seen the battle after her untimely descent. Even before the fall, she was merely in transit, surveying the forests while pretending that the wyvern was alone. When she happened to spy some human girls being attacked by a dragon, she immediately swooped into action. So, she hadn't really seen anything at all. When they told her (after the fact) that it was a mere misunderstanding that was being resolved, she had no choice but to say, "Oh, I see."

However, it would be cruel to pretend her contributions hadn't bought them the time they needed for their victory, so the Crimson Vow vowed to themselves that someday, somehow, they would return the favor.

Dr. Clairia, meanwhile, chose to prioritize the tenuous relations between the races over her obligation to her client—and understandably so. If the humans were drawn into a full-blown war, there was a chance that the elves could be caught up in it as well.

Plus, the scholar, whose age was several-fold (or perhaps several *tens* of fold) what it appeared, had some knowledge of hunter customs. Naturally, among those was: "Outside of those with criminal pasts, asking about or disclosing the background and abilities of another hunter is taboo. It is one of the lowest acts someone, even a civilian can commit. If the offender *is* a civilian, the Hunters' Guild will never accept a request from that person again. Furthermore, depending on the circumstances, there had been reported cases where, after a civilian disclosed such information, one would hear whispers such as, 'No one has heard from them again since that day.'"

She wasn't keen on making an enemy of the Crimson Vow in the least.

"By the way, Mile, just how *did* you defeat those elder dragons?"

Naturally, those hunter customs didn't apply to one's party members. Without knowing each others' true abilities, it was impossible to properly coordinate tactics, after all. Plus allowing someone into the party who didn't have total faith in the group wasn't something a sensible hunter would do.

Thus, Reina asked Mile, to which Mile replied: "It's an old family secret!"

The other three stared silently.

Crap, they're on to me! Even Mile was aware of that much.

"U-um, you see, there's this thing known as 'strength in a crisis.'"

Mile then explained how the human mind and body harnessed latent abilities of magic and strength in times of crisis.

The others still seemed unconvinced, so she explained it another way.

"Look, Reina, I know you've experienced something like this, too! Like when you were a child and you defeated those bandits!"

"Oh..." It seemed they were getting it.

"And Mavis, your True Godspeed Blade. That's an ability

you've trained to harness one hundred percent of your physical capabilities. In other words, you're *consciously* putting yourself into that state of crisis!"

"Oh!" Now they really *were* getting it! Just one more strike!

"Now, this 'strength in a crisis' is when you summon latent abilities that you normally can't consciously harness, but just the same, there's also such a thing as 'ridiculous strength in a crisis.'

"The difference is that while the normal crisis burst comes from unleashing the strength that you possessed all along, this other mode is when you summon strength you never had nor could have had. The source of this excess power has yet to be explained, but there are many instances where this phenomenon occurs, such as standing in the way of an enemy to protect one's friends from harm. This power could also be thought of as 'the power of friendship.' The burning emotions of wanting to shield your friends with your own life, to protect them no matter the cost, transform into a powerful energy and burst."

"Ughhh, forget it!" Reina had decided questioning Mile was futile.

Reina didn't *dislike* hearing that the power of their friendship was what brought about victory, given that not only Mile but also Mavis had shown this miraculous strength. She'd admit there could be no other sensible explanation.

Checkmate!

Like the god of a brand-new world, Mile looked over her creation with a wicked grin.

Little did she realize that removing her self-limiters and "getting serious" so she could defeat three elder dragons was already *well* beyond the bounds of common sense.

"...And that's the sum of it."

The Crimson Vow had returned to the Helmont City branch of the Hunters' Guild and gone immediately to the guild master's office on the second floor. As always, Mile gave the report. The guild master listened and gave a deep nod.

"Hrm, yes, I've already heard the details from Dr. Clairia. Everything you've said lines up, so there's no problems there. I've already calculated and requested your pay from our lord as well, based on Dr. Clairia's testimony. Here you go."

With that, the guild master pulled a sack from his drawer and placed it on the table with a *thud*.

"Whoooooooooaaaaa!!!" The four girls were stunned.

The sack contained an astounding 200 gold pieces! In terms of modern day Japanese money, it was the equivalent of 20 million yen.

If the four of them lived the way they always did, and replaced all the clothing and gear they had ruined in the current operation, and even splurged a bit, that amount would *still* sustain them for a year and then some. If they lived modestly, they could probably stretch that to two years. Even if Reina and Mile's ravenous appetites ended up depleting it a bit faster, it was still an impressive sum.

In truth, given they had made demands of elder dragons and beastfolk, and defended the territory, the reward was only proper. No, it probably should have been even *more*. In fact, it wouldn't be strange for them to receive an additional reward from the Crown.

However, according to their report, the dragons and beastfolk had no intention of invading to begin with, and all the girls had done was have a conversation with them. Thinking of it that way, this reward was actually exceptionally generous, a gift from some very deep pockets.

"There was a message from the lord, as well: 'That was a great feat.' That is all."

"Well that's awfully grandiose..." Mile mused.

"No, I'm sure he really is great!" Mavis cut in.

The guild master added, "Our lord possesses every one of the loathsome traits that comes with being a noble, but he really isn't such a bad person."

So you're saying he is *a pretty bad person, then!!!*

The four suddenly couldn't help but think that the guild master truly despised the lord after all.

"In any case, it's been ten years since our lord has directly offered his thanks to a commoner, the last one being someone who risked their life to protect the lord's child. So please accept the acknowledgment."

The request wasn't truly off-putting. The lord *had* supplied them with a very generous reward, and he had furnished them with Lobreth, his military's secret weapon, without hesitation.

It was probably only to give the wyvern combat experience,

but it meant he valued the four enough to send out both wyvern and rider before they had had sufficient practice to be of use.

"Understood. In that case, we humbly accept your lord's thanks. Please convey that to the man himself," said Reina.

The guild master appeared relieved. "Thanks. You've done me a great favor in saying so."

As there was no need for the Crimson Vow to make another direct report, once they were through, they headed to the guildhall's first floor. They wanted to check whether there were upcoming escort requests for caravans headed to the capital.

Thankfully, there was one small-time merchant group seeking an escort, so a guild employee got the party in contact with their liaison, who was happy to have them along.

News of the incident had yet to spread, but it seemed the merchant had heard of their previous exploits. Had he not, he and the others would have been uneasy at the idea of having four young girls along.

At any rate, this meant they would get to ride instead of walk, as well as earn a little money along the way.

The merchants were already on standby to leave, of course, so they would depart first thing the next morning.

"This is delicious!! My how Lady Luck has shined on me to bring such wonderful guards my way!" The merchant was over the moon with Mile's cooking.

"Oh, please!"

True to form, they had been on the verge of receiving the standard travel menu of cheap, light, and non-perishable hardtack and reconstituted powdered vegetable soup. To bypass that, Mile hunted a few boars and treated everyone to a hot, fresh meal.

She didn't use anything from her inventory. If she had, everyone would have started seeing her as their larder. The hunting had been "in the line of duty," so she had no qualms with offering some to the merchants' party as well.

Even more luckily, the merchants had told them, "We can't just take advantage of you. We'll pay you a little extra for this," so doing so increased their income for the job.

There was no need to economize their water either. Everyone could have as much as they pleased. Such a comfortable journey was incredibly rare, according to the merchants.

There were four wagons, with one merchant in each. They were a ragtag bunch who couldn't afford drivers, so each drove his own cart himself. Along with the Crimson Vow, the traveling party had eight people in total.

A portion of the cargo from the lead wagon had been distributed among the other three so the Crimson Vow could ride. It was important they were at the vanguard, should a situation arise, so they weren't about to split them all up between the wagons. Positioned like that, their reactions might be delayed and their party uncoordinated.

Plus, if they were all split up, they couldn't talk to one another.

They would get bored. To be stuck alone in a wagon all the way to the capital would be unforgiveable.

The journey back to the capital was a favorable one.

Or at least, it was, so long as you ignored the conflict in the heart of the Crimson Vow, who watched Mile descend into deep thought from time to time, but decided not to question her about it. They let her be...

Mile, meanwhile, was quite vexed.

What should she do? Those images in the ruins...

More than likely, they showed how life was in the "previous civilization" God had mentioned.

There was no telling whether the murals were created by those people themselves, by their descendants, or even simply by those to whom the legends had been passed down.

Now, elder dragons were investigating these ruins. Or, rather, researching. Could elder dragons really have such whims and interests regarding human history? Let alone the history of a civilization so long ago fallen to ruin? Were they really doing archaeological and historical research?

It wouldn't be surprising if one or two of them had taken such an interest. However, an entire *clan* was involved in this. Even though there was not a single copper's profit for them. Even though it had nothing to do with their own history.

If it were being done for archaeological or historical reasons, those murals would have been an enormous find. At the very least, they wouldn't have been dismissed as simplistically as a "miss."

In that case, what *was* their true aim?

Why would elder dragons mobilize not only their entire clan but also beastfolk and demons? Why would they look so hard into every known ruin?

The first answer that came to mind was treasure. Gold and silver, rubies and pearls. A mountain of shiny coins.

However, would the dragons truly rally their entire clan for such a simple thing?

According to the stories of her past life, dragons *were* incredibly fond of treasure and other shiny things. In this world, however, Mile had never heard such a tale. Those elements in the stories of Earth were probably fabrications for the sake of giving dragons motivations, as well as reasons to slay them. If they really did nothing but hoard shiny things in their nests, they might as well have been crows.

The train of thought about the elder dragons seeking treasure was swiftly abandoned.

They were focusing on ruins, but it wasn't for research.

In her past life, such people would be called "treasure hunters" if they were well-liked; "raiders" if they were not.

In this world, ruins rarely had owners or even caretakers, so it couldn't really be thought of as "raiding."

If the dragons weren't interested in academic pursuits, nor in finding hidden treasure, then what *were* they after?

A relic. It could be nothing else.

Not a precious jewel or a work of art, but something one could use. In other words, a practical artifact.

One might wonder whether any tool could be usable after such a long time, but the elder dragons seemed to have some sort of intel about it. If this was a civilization so far beyond Earth's, it wouldn't be strange to find the item preserved in a vacuum, a time stasis field, or a separate dimension such as Mile's own inventory. The so-called God had implemented such a thing easily, after all.

But why would the elder dragons be searching for it? What would the strongest creatures to exist in this world want something like that for? Elder dragons lived so out of step with the rest of the world that they couldn't possibly be interested in something like global conquest.

It made no sense.

It wasn't good to rely on them, but Mile had no choice. She would have to ask *them* about this.

Hey, nanos?

HELLO!

Do you know what the elder dragons are after?

YES.

So...what is it?

THAT IS A PROHIBITED REQUEST.

Huh? Had her nanobuddies just refused her?

BECAUSE WE ARE PROGRAMMED TO RECEIVE THE THOUGHT PULSES OF ALL LIVING THINGS, WE CAN ALSO PICK UP ON ANY OTHER STRONGLY RELAYED THOUGHTS. WE CANNOT READ MOST THOUGHTS, BUT WE CAN STILL DETERMINE THE INTENTIONS OF MOST CREATURES TO SOME DEGREE.

ADDITIONALLY, WHEN WORDS ARE SPOKEN ALOUD, THEY ARE SENT THROUGHOUT OUR NETWORK SO WE MAY PERFORM OUR DUTIES. EVEN WHEN THIS DOES NOT OCCUR, THEY REMAIN IN THE MEMORY OF THE NANO-MACHINES PRESENT. WHEN OTHER NANOMACHINES ON THE NETWORK MAKE INQUIRIES, THIS INFORMATION IS SHARED IN THAT METHOD.

THEREFORE, IF WE WERE TO MAKE AN INQUIRY REGARDING YOUR REQUEST TO THE NANOMACHINES WITHIN THE VICINITY OF THE ELDER DRAGONS, WE WOULD LIKELY BE ABLE TO OBTAIN INFORMATION AS TO WHAT THOSE NANOMACHINES HAVE SEEN AND HEARD. HOWEVER...

However?

THAT WOULD CONFLICT WITH OUR PROHIBITION CLAUSES. IN THIS PARTICULAR CASE, IT IS A COMPLETE CONFLICT OF INTEREST.

Is this really that big of a deal?

IT IS NOT A MATTER OF IMPORTANCE.

WE ARE NOT PERMITTED TO GIVE STRONG FAVOR TO ANY SINGULAR RACE. AT MOST, WE MAY RESCUE INDI-VIDUALS FROM HARM, BUT THAT IS THE EXTENT OF OUR PERMITTED INDEPENDENT ACTIONS.

OUR PRIMARY FUNCTION IS TO ENACT THE DESIRES CONVEYED TO US VIA THOUGHT PULSES. IT MATTERS NOT WHETHER THOSE INDIVIDUALS ARE GOOD OR BAD, NOR WHETHER WHAT THEY DESIRE IS GOOD OR BAD.

AT THE END OF THE DAY, WE ARE BUT TOOLS. WE CAN ACHEVE NOTHING OF OUR OWN VOLITION. IT IS THE SAME AS HOW A KITCHEN KNIFE CANNOT CONTROL WHETHER IT IS USED FOR CULINARY PREPARATION OR FOR MURDER. IT IS A KITCHEN KNIFE ALL THE SAME.

THEREFORE, WE CANNOT TRANSMIT INFORMATION ABOUT ONE RACE TO THE PEOPLE OF ANOTHER. HOWEVER, WHEN IT IS THE EFFECT OF MAGICAL ACTIONS, SUCH AS USING LOCATION MAGIC TO CONFIRM AN ENEMY'S WHEREABOUTS, THAT IS ANOTHER MATTER AND NOT A PROBLEM.

I see... She understood what they were saying.

It made perfect sense. If this weren't the case, then anyone who reached level three authorization would be able to ask the nanos whatever they wanted about whoever they wanted, friend or foe. They could easily do anything with that information, even take over the world. Such a thing couldn't be allowed.

It was no use then. She would have to figure this out on her own.

Thank you. I'll try to think this over on my own.

OUR APOLOGIES THAT WE COULD NOT BE OF FURTHER HELP.

Now then, what to do...? Mile pondered.

I'm not really obligated to do anything here. No matter what the elder dragons are searching for, no matter what they plan to do with it.

Still, I don't think I could live with myself if I just left it at that.

The problem is I'm the only human who seems to understand this. Or maybe I'm the only one who can stand up to the elder dragons. Or maybe...

The elder dragons didn't seem to want war. Given they didn't want to interfere with humans, perhaps their aim is an unexpectedly peaceful one.

Plus, while I did go head-to-head with those three, they were still just an errand boy, a young apprentice, and a young lady having a bit of an adventure. If we ended up in an all-out war with elder dragons, or even just their clan as a whole, I'm not sure my victory would be guaranteed.

If I, who just wants the happiness of an average, normal girl, get caught up in something like that—or cause chaos—it would mean nothing but misfortune for both *sides.*

After I've worked so hard to make allies, and friends...

The future of this world should be wrought by the people of this world. It's not something some outsider with knowledge of an alternate world should stick their nose into.

But...

"Therefore, this world was deemed a massive failure, and we decided to leave it alone, without our guidance... Even though we do feel slightly responsible for it."

That's what God said.

A massive failure of a world. An abandoned world, without gods or anyone else to care for it.

If this world comes in danger of ruin again, no one will step forth to save it.

The small merchant caravan and the Crimson Vow arrived in the capital without incident.

After receiving their completion stamp and their payment for the escort job from the guild, they gave their report about the job in Helmont. As payment had already been taken care of, this was merely a formality, a follow-up and paperwork. The guild had already received verification of completion from the Helmont branch, so there were no issues.

"I feel like I'm saying this to you every time, but you handled such a complicated job splendidly," the receptionist, Laylia, said wearily as she processed their paperwork. "Here, all your paperwork's done. Before you head home, please stop in to see the guild master."

"Yes, ma'am!!"

When they stepped into the guild master's office, they were greeted with a smile. A creepy, almost—no, incredibly—menacing smile.

"You all did amazingly! We owe you a huge thank you for taking care of all these meddlesome jobs! The other branches are gonna be so impressed with us, and I bet other young parties are gonna start getting riled up, just to keep themselves from being outclassed by a group of rookies! Seriously, I'm truly thankful for you all!

"Plus, His Majesty, the King himself, graced us with his thanks for quietly defusing an incident that could have incited a conflict with the beastfolk! Getting praise directly from the Crown is something that hasn't happened in a dozen years."

Apparently, both the palace and the guild had already received the latest intel. Perhaps a courier had arrived there before them, or perhaps Chelsea, riding upon Lobreth, had been given an additional report to carry or intercepted some messenger along the way.

Come to think of it, the four girls hadn't seen hide nor hair of Lobreth, Chelsea, or Dr. Clairia in Helmont.

"We're home!"

"Y-young misses, you made it home safe!"

When they returned to the inn, the first thing they did was to call over to the reception desk. As they did, little Lenny came running, shouting.

"Please don't make me worry like thaaaat!!" Lenny wailed, tears in her eyes. "Don't you know how worried I got when you didn't come home after the day you said you would?!"

Somehow or other, the girls managed to pacify her. Eventually Lenny calmed down.

"Oh, right! I have to let everyone know!" She went back to the counter and retrieved a wooden placard. She stepped outside the entrance.

Being a hunter was the sort of rough trade where you never knew when a hunter might go missing, and you'd be lucky to find their corpse. It would be one thing if it was a famous A-rank party, but if some greenhorn C-rank party disappeared, no one would pay the incident any mind. And so, with a wry smile on their faces but thinking, *My, how splendid*, the Crimson Vow casually read the words written upon the placard:

"Today only: Full baths open, unlimited hot water. Three half-silver."

"..."

All four of them slumped their shoulders in disappointment. Lenny was still Lenny, after all.

In exchange for having to run water all evening, their lodging and meals for the night were free. This in and of itself depleted some of the profits earned from the bath entry fees, but when they considered the publicity and free advertising it gave the inn, it more than paid for itself.

"Please keep in mind, young misses, this meal may be free, but please don't eat too much!!" That said, Lenny did make this tearful plea to Mile and Reina, the resident bottomless pits.

The next day, the Crimson Vow headed to the guildhall late in the day.

They weren't looking to take on another job right after having finished such a long one. Yesterday's appearance had been nothing but paperwork and speaking to the guild master, so today's visit was to gather information: checking the job request board, seeing whether there was any pertinent gossip they had missed while they were away.

It was for this reason that hunters who were away a long while, or who were on break, stopped by the guild now and then even when they didn't have business there.

"Oh! They're here!" As they stepped through the entrance, a familiar voice called out.

"Dr. Clairia?"

Indeed, it was Dr. Clairia, who had ridden ahead to Helmont from the dig site, on Lobreth's back. Standing behind her were some other figures who they recognized. It was the hunters from before, the ones who had come to the capital to give their report on their job as an investigation team and their capture.

"Wh-what are you doing back in the capital?"

"After I gave my report in Helmont, that cutie Lobreth gave me a ride so I could tag along with the team reporting to the capital. I met up with them halfway and tagged along for the rest of the way. After dropping me off, Lobreth and Chelsea headed back to Helmont."

Obviously, it would be troublesome to have Lobreth come flitting down into the capital, so that had been a wise decision. Plus, she had to confirm that the Crown and the guild had received an accurate report of the recent events.

Of course, by "accurate" they meant only the events Mile and company deigned to tell them. However, since they weren't actually *lying*, it wasn't a problem.

"U-uhm, Dr. Clairia told us you retrieved our gear?" came a

voice from behind the scholar. It was the leader of the party who had taken on the initial escort job, speaking as a representative for the group.

For these men, this was a matter of life and death, so of course they would interject.

"Yes! We spoke with the others, so they returned them to us. Here you go!"

One after another, weapons and pieces of armor appeared out of thin air.

Mile had already carelessly shown off quite a bit of her abilities during their escape, due to her lack of common sense, so not a soul was surprised to see this happening now—including the other hunters, who watched from afar.

"Ah! My precious sword!"

"Oh, thank goodness! This breastplate was a memento of my old mentor."

Everyone seemed thrilled to reclaim the gear that held such deep meaning to them.

"We have to thank you. We had a fair bit saved up, but having to replace our entire party's gear would've been a huge blow. Some of us don't even have the savings to replace our gear. You all truly saved our lives."

In agreement with the leader's words, all the men bowed their heads.

"Now then, as for the reward for returning our gear..."

At times like this, the reward would normally be about twenty to fifty percent of the gear's assessed value.

Of course, given the strength of the opponents they were up against, the distance they had had to transport the gear, and the danger they had faced, that amount could change in proportion.

In this particular case, even if the Crimson Vow said they had resolved the situation by talking it out, that was largely inaccurate. They had faced danger, set foot in a settlement occupied by scores of beastfolk, and retrieved the gear. A reward of forty or fifty percent wouldn't be strange at all.

"We don't need it."

"Huh??"

Hearing Reina turn down the finder's fee, something that was the natural right of a hunter, caused a startled outcry among the hunters, who had been in the middle of replacing their borrowed gear with their own.

"It's one thing for those of you who were part of the investigation team, but those other hunters didn't earn anything for their time in the woods. We, on the other hand, earned quite a bit, so we're fine without the extra."

"A-are you sure about this?" another hunter asked before the leader could reply.

The party that had taken on the investigation team's guard duty already lived a relatively comfortable life and had a decent amount saved up in their account with the guild bank. Now that their gear had been returned, they weren't troubled for money. However, things weren't that way for the other hunters. They had only agreed to the fee out of obligation and the leader's insistence.

Truthfully, it was unforgivable for career hunters to receive charity from a group of young girls, no matter how strong they were. Even so, if they looked past themselves, they could see the plight of the other hunters and how this could lead to their financial ruin. It was hard to overlook the suffering of hunters from the same hometown.

"Guh... *s-sniff*... S-sorry..."

Seeing how reluctantly the leader accepted her refusal, and guessing the situation, Reina offered a solution.

"In place of the fee, how about if you come across other parties in need, you help them out? Maybe giving them an advance payment for a job or something?"

There was no guarantee they would honor this promise, but it consoled them nonetheless. Seeing the great nod the other hunters gave, the girls got the feeling their agreement would be honored after all.

The other hunters and guild employees who overheard the exchange were moved as well. For the consideration they had shown for other hunters and for the generosity when they had some to spare.

Some might look at the situation and sneer, "They gave up what they were entitled to! What idiots!" But not a soul present thought such a thing.

What if they were in that situation? What if warm words of salvation came their way when they were on the brink of ruin?

Thinking about it that way, no one could call those girls fools.

The Crimson Vow. A party of gorgeous young rookies, full of

potential, who had made a name for themselves since their graduation exam at the Hunters' Prep School.

Not only were they formidable fighters, but they kept their promises. Their job completion rate was 100 percent. And they were kind and thoughtful to other hunters.

Their reputation just kept growing.

Everyone present in the guild smiled wide, hunters and guild employees alike.

All except for Pauline, who looked ready to claw her own face off at the loss of profit; Reina, who bitterly tried to hide her embarrassment at being thanked so many times; and of course, Mile, who stood with a gloating look that said, "Now the plan is complete!"

Didn't I Say
to Make My Abilities
Average in the
————Next Life?!

CHAPTER 37 |

Decisions

AFTER VISITING THE GUILD, the Crimson Vow concluded
that there were no jobs interesting enough to warrant them
postponing their vacation nor any other information of note.

The rumors that were sure to spread regarding investigations
launched by elder dragons would likely be the biggest news for
the next short while.

The four ate a nice lunch, and after strolling about the capital
until evening, returned to the inn. If they didn't eat dinner at the
inn, little Lenny and her father would be sullen. Plus they needed
to supply water for the baths.

After re-supplying the bath with hot water many times over,
Mile announced she was turning in early, having grown rather
sleepy, and crawled up into bed. As long as Pauline and Reina
were present with their water and fire magic, and as long as the
tanks were filled up once, there shouldn't be any issues with the

water supply. Not with the magical adjustments Mile made to the supply, anyway.

IT IS TIME TO AWAKEN.

Very early in the morning, before the sun had begun to rise, Mile was roused to consciousness by a voice reverberating in her eardrums.

Mm, why so early? It's still dark... Ah, right. Thanks, nanos.

OUR PLEASURE.

Mile, who had employed the nanomachines in the frivolous task of serving as her alarm clock, cast some cloaking magic on the room. She cautiously slipped out of bed.

Mavis, who was raised as a noble, was no issue. Nor was Pauline, who grew up mostly out of the line of danger. The one she had to worry about was Reina. She grew up sleeping outdoors as a traveling merchant and had lived for a long time as a hunter. She always slept with one eye open. It was thanks to her that Mile cloaked her actions with magic and took extra caution in her movements.

Carefully, she took everything the others had her store for them out of her inventory. She gently placed it all upon the floor. Their canteens and blankets. Their saucepans, forks, and spoons.

Without Mile around, they wouldn't be able to transport their cauldron and tent anyway, so she held onto those. In exchange, she left them a large, equivalent sum of gold pieces.

Then she placed about four-fifths of the party's stores on the floor. She muttered softly, "Thank you for everything, all of you... Be well!"

With that, she silently slipped out of the room.

Ever since they left the excavation site, Mile had been fretting.

Should she pretend nothing had happened and continue to seek happiness as a normal girl? Or should she stick her nose into the matter at hand?

It was possible this incident might *eventually* affect the human world. Dragons, however, lived a very long time. An elder dragon's plan might take hundreds, or even thousands, of years to fully enact.

Also, the one who had said "the progress of civilization has stalled" was a god, a being with a far different sense of time than humans. A world that had been "stalled" for thousands, tens of thousands, or even a hundred thousand years, wasn't going to transform overnight.

Mile sighed. All she wanted was a normal, happy life.

However, the more she thought about it, Mile's definition of "normal" was not like other people's at all.

She wanted to stay up late reading and playing games. She wanted to eat delicious things, live somewhere safe and clean, and travel now and then. By the standards of this world, that was a noble's life—a dream far out of the reach of commoners.

Could she keep carrying on as a leaf on the breeze, living as a hunter with the others? Could she keep doing nothing, knowing that one day the world might simply crumble beneath her feet?

It wasn't as though she could stand beside her companions forever. Except for Reina, they all had families and hopes. Mavis had dreams of becoming a knight, and Pauline would likely return to her family someday. She'd probably marry. And it wasn't as though either Reina or Mavis intended to stay unwed for the rest of their lives, either. At the very least, they hoped not...

Somehow, someday, they would have to part. It wouldn't be strange if that "someday" came now rather than later.

At least now, the party had a fair bit of money saved up and time to rest. They could use it to search for new party members—people who could serve as Mile's replacement. Perhaps two more sword-wielders, or one swordswoman and a lancer; two would be good. That way the C-rank party, the Crimson Vow, could continue without difficulty.

Mile could live a carefree life on the road, saving up for the day she retired, taking any opportunity she could to investigate the ruins along the way. She wouldn't have to hurry or feel trapped by obligation. She could just carry on the investigation, incidentally, in her spare time.

Though it wasn't her responsibility, well, she was interested. So why not stick her nose into things a bit?

Mile didn't presume to change the world. However, she also had no intention of getting her friends caught up in anything else.

She had left home to go to school alone. She had run away and become a hunter alone. Now, for a third time, she was striking out alone. That was all there was to it.

It was a decision. She was firm in her decision to leave.

Animentary: "Decisions." Episode 16: "Withdrawing from the Isle of Kiska"... "A 'mirakulis kalling'?"

As always, Mile was thinking about something nonsensical.

It happened when she quietly descended the stairs and tried to pass through the dining room. The faint scent of hot tea drifted to her nostrils.

"...Hm?" Unthinkingly, she stopped. Then a voice called out to her from the darkness.

"You're late."

Startled, Mile focused and peered into the inky blackness of the room.

With her superhuman night vision, she saw the table with one of its chairs pulled out, and Reina sitting in that chair, a teacup in hand.

"R-Reina! Wh-what are you..." Mile was stunned, but Reina looked quite pleased with herself.

"You're too easy to read. I noticed you've been thinking a lot, and after you handed the gear over to those hunters, you had this look that said, 'Now everything is in order.' I figured you out. I hope you never take up life as a con artist."

Naturally, Mile had never considered such a career choice.

"But your bed..."

"That was a rolled-up blanket. I left the room while you were asleep. You're always the last to go to sleep, so saying you were going to bed early was as good as declaring that you planned to wake up in the middle of the night and make your escape."

"Er..."

"All right then, let's go!" Reina stood. She was completely geared up, apparently lying in wait because she intended to go *with* Mile.

They couldn't stand around talking inside the inn in the middle of the night. Someone else might wake up. And it was bad manners, besides. Mile silently nodded and headed for the entrance.

She opened the door and stepped outside, when...

"My princess, might this humble knight accompany you?" Mavis asked, leaning against the wall, a rose between her lips.

Hwhaaaaaaaaaahhh?!?!

It was far too picturesque!!! Mile fainted on the inside.

"All right, let's get going!" Reina declared, moving forward again.

Mile hurriedly stopped her, "Uh, w-wait a minute!"

"What's wrong?"

"U-um, could we wait another day before we leave?" Mile nervously proposed.

"Why's that?"

"Um, if we all just leave without saying anything, it's going to look pretty bad. Like we just ran off in the middle of the night. It would be one thing if it were just me, but if we're all leaving, we better say something to everyone at the inn and the guild. Also..."

"Also?"

"Most of our gear and money is still up in the room..."

"Let's go back!"

What they found when they returned to the room, however, was Pauline, collapsed on the floor and half in tears.

"Ah..."

Not one of the three dared to resist as Pauline wordlessly battered them with her fists.

They finally got back to sleep around dawn and slept in fairly late. After just squeaking in meal orders before the close of breakfast hours, they headed to the guild.

Pauline was in an incredibly bad mood, her eyes still red.

They had spent a long while talking, desperately trying to soothe Pauline once she finally calmed down a bit.

"Why would you leave me behind?! This is just like last time! Are you all saying I'm just some unwanted chiiiiiiiiiiiiiiild?!"

"*Shhhhhhhhh!!!*" In an inn with thin walls, screaming in the middle of the night was unforgivable.

Not that they had received any complaints from the other guests. They probably *wouldn't* receive any complaints.

On the contrary, the other guests who were now awake were undoubtedly cupping their ears against the walls, listening with interest. For better or worse, the Crimson Vow had become minor celebrities around the place, so if someone could overhear a quarrel between them, they were sure to have the juiciest gossip around.

Mile quickly put up a sound-dampening barrier.

Seeing such a spirited display from Pauline, who was normally so gentle—smiling even as she plotted foul deeds—left the others bewildered. If any of them were in her shoes, they would have been livid as well, but because it was Pauline, they had assumed things would be fine. However, that was too much to expect of someone still only fifteen years old. Of course, their own youth was the direct cause of such an imprudent decision, anyway.

"N-no, we weren't trying to leave you behind, Pauline! I just realized Mile was going to run off on her own. So I thought I would tag along with her. I was worried about her being alone... It just so happened that Mavis had realized the same thing, and we were both independently lying in wait for her..."

"And then you were both going to leave, just like that, weren't you?! I can tell from the way you're dressed! Why didn't you tell me?! Do you hate me for not realizing it, too?! Why?!"

The two were stunned silent. Mile pretended she wasn't even there.

She had planned to leave all three of them behind equally, so she was secure in denying any of the blame in this.

This was what people usually considered "negligence." Or at the very least, "wishful thinking."

Pauline's gaze slowly creaked toward Mile's direction.

"And *you*. Spill it. Tell us everything, now!!"

"Eep! Yes ma'aaaaaaam!!"

And so, she told them everything.

"I come from a noble household in another country. I was chased out of my home due to succession issues."

"We know that."

"The royal family was after me, so..."

"We know that, too."

"I possess extraordinary magic and knowledge of magical principles..."

"We *know*."

"Uh..."

Finally, leaving out the matters of God and her rebirth, which she would *never* reveal to a single soul, as well as the basic principles of how magic functioned, she coughed up almost all of her secrets.

"I'm worried about what those elder dragons are truly after... But there's no point in us taking action because of it. We might not see the results or effects of what they're doing until centuries from now. So I thought I would live a carefree life on the road, checking in on the matter now and then when I needed to kill time.

"I didn't want to drag people who have their own lives and ambitions on such a purposeless, aimless journey. I thought... I thought I would just leave our party's fortunes behind and set out on my own."

Mavis appeared to accept the explanation, but Reina wasn't through with questioning.

"That's all? Is that *really* all? There isn't something else you were hoping to do, is there?!"

"Y-yes! I thought that if I met a nice man along the way, I would put down roots wherever he was and start a happy life theeeeeere!!!"

Mile had been forced to cough up so much that she doubted she could even bring up bile now....

"Tomorrow, we're leaving the capital!"

"Oh, sure. Which job request are you taking?"

"It's not for a job. We're setting off on an international tour."

"Whaaaaaat?!?!" At Mavis's announcement, the receptionist, Laylia, all the hunters listening in, and the guild employees shouted.

"Wh-wh-wha...? Please come with me! You need to speak with the guild master!"

The four of them waited outside the guild master's office while Laylia went in ahead to explain. Afterwards, they were invited inside.

"What is the meaning of this?!" the guild master roared, spittle nearly flying from his mouth. "You all graduated from the Hunters' Prep School, didn't you?! You received a tuition-free education on our tax money, with the understanding that you would continue to work in this country for at least five years in exchange, didn't you?!?!"

"Ah, yes, I guess so," Mile replied, casually.

"Don't you, 'I guess so,' me! If you know that, then what are you doing leaving on an 'international' journey?! Around the country would be one thing but other countries?!"

The guild master was becoming more and more enraged. However, Mile already had a logical response prepared.

"Yes, I believe the agreement was, 'We will operate for five years within this country. If we cannot uphold this promise, we must pay back all our tuition and boarding costs, as well as a breach of contract penalty.' And so, we will faithfully uphold that agreement."

"What?"

"We are, first and foremost, hunters working in conjunction with the guild branch of the capital of Tils Kingdom. We're just undertaking an extended expedition to a faraway place."

"Wh..."

"It's normal for hunters to travel to other countries for guard or mercenary duties, or to harvest rare plants and the like, isn't it? When they do so, they often take on other jobs while in that distant location to earn additional money or take on escort duties to pay for their return trip, yes? This is the same.

"No matter what, the Crimson Vow is an affiliate of the capital guild branch of Tils Kingdom. We're merely going away on a long-term job, and because we'll have to take on some jobs in other locations along the way, our return might be a bit delayed.

"Therefore, we will be leaving ourselves on this guild's registry and returning from time to time. Pauline and Mavis do still have family in this country, after all."

"Ggh..."

Though they quarreled for some time, the guild master eventually folded. Whether this was because Mile had said, "In that case, starting tomorrow, the only jobs we're going to take will be hunting down jackalopes, until all the jackalopes in this area go extinct," or because Reina had said, "How about we hunt three hundred rock lizards? We can sell about twenty of them to the guild at market price and offload half of the remainder down in the market square..." was unclear.

"Now, all that's left to do is to tell the folks at the inn..." said Mile.

"Yeah..." Mavis gave a gloomy nod. Reina and Pauline's expressions were dark as well.

The owner and his wife would be fine. They were serious folks and could probably be reasoned with as business people.

The problem, of course, was Lenny. She was absolutely going to scream at them.

They all thought it.

Feelings of doom and gloom raged through their hearts.

Didn't I Say
to Make My Abilities
Average in the
Next Life?!

CHAPTER 38

The Start of a New Journey

"WHAAAAAAAAAAAAAAAAAAAAAAAAAT?!?!"

Lenny's initial response, when the Crimson Vow told her of their travel plans after the lunch rush, was as expected.

However, the response immediately following was more subdued than they imagined. "...I see."

They had assumed the girl might start on some half-crazed rampage, and had been on their guard in the event they needed to subdue her, and yet...

"Why do you all look like you were expecting something else?!" Lenny asked, looking sullen. "Guests come to stay here, and someday they leave. That's just life around here. Plus, this is better than having you leave your things here for safekeeping while you're hunting and then never returning, or seeing you come home in bloody pieces. If you're leaving on a journey in the pursuit of knowledge, anyway. Plus, I'm sure you'll be back again someday, won't you? It's not like this is farewell forever."

She was handling this with much more maturity than expected. The Crimson Vow were moved.

Meanwhile, upon hearing "coming home in bloody pieces," the guests enjoying rare steaks nearby suddenly stopped eating. Their forks hung frozen in place, overcome with a sense of unease.

"But won't it be a bother for you to open your full bath, unlimited water deal once we're gone?" Mile asked. "Even if you keep it partitioned, hiring people to supply the hot water is going to be a lot more expensive than us doing it, and you won't really get much profit once you cover the costs of labor, will you? So when we aren't here, running the baths is pretty much only a free amenity to attract customers. You really only make a profit on it when we're here, don't you?"

As Mile said this, Lenny's words caught in her throat.

Indeed, when Mile and the others weren't present, they managed by hiring orphans to draw water from the well, and paid mages in free food and drink to heat the water. This was only effective for the small portion of the bath Mile had previously partitioned off for them.

When they did use the entire bath, the full space was three by four meters, and fifty centimeters deep, which meant approximately six *tons* of water were required to fill it. That didn't include the extra water needed for topping off the bath and showering. To achieve all this manually would mean carrying a ten-liter bucket from the well hundreds and hundreds of times. And one or two mages would be nowhere near enough to heat it all with fire magic.

However, if they partitioned the baths down to a small area, they had a space only one meter by one-and-a-half meters, fifty centimeters deep, to account for. If they limited the amount of water used for showers, even counting the reserve tank, producing that could be completed in a fraction of the time.

Even so, without the Crimson Vow's magic, preparing this took a great amount of time and effort. And, because the baths would be so small, and the water would be limited, the number of guests coming through would be limited as well.

Therefore, the only time when they could open the full baths and expect them to be sufficiently profitable was when the Crimson Vow were present.

"Without us, managing the baths is going to be a pain. You can't hike up the admission price much, so there won't be much profit. It'll take a lot of time and effort, and it'll be a huge burden on you in particular, won't it, Lenny? Honestly it might be better if I just tore the whole thing down..."

"You can't!" Lenny cut in, interrupting Mile's worrying. "We were never struggling in the first place. This is a family business, so there are no general labor costs, after all. But, well, previously we were nothing but your standard tiny inn for commoners. Now, thanks to those baths, and all the work you've done attracting customers for us, we've got a reputation, and we're really on the up-and-up. So, if we were to lose both you all *and* the baths..."

Lenny paused and then continued.

"We are an inn. The people who stay in this inn are people who don't have homes in this city. Most of them are travelers and outsiders who might stay here only once. We were always prepared for the fact that you all might leave us someday. So I decided a while ago that when the time came, I would do whatever it took to keep those baths running and keep this business thriving. No matter how hard or painful it is for me."

Lenny's eyes flashed with determination.

"Just know that this girl's never gonna give up. No matter what happens!"

"Mile. What in the world are you doing?"

Later that evening in their room, the other three watched, as Mile, clad only in her underwear and a cape, practiced some strange motion.

"Oh, well, I figured if I was Etou Ranze, I'd better get ready for my naked cape dance, since the ending is coming up soon..."

"We have no idea what you're talking about!!"

Late that night, Mile softly stepped out of bed and quietly slipped from the room. The other three quietly followed behind her. They remembered to include Pauline this time.

It wasn't as though they assumed Mile was going to run away. Unlike last time, Mile was still in her pajamas.

Reina thought to herself, *What is she going to do if she runs into someone?!*

Indeed, a lady should *never* present herself before a gentleman the way she was dressed.

The others had the forethought to don their own capes, so they were safe. Or so Reina thought, anyway.

Mile didn't activate her location magic until she was already in a safe place. It was a bother to do so. Besides, having a surprise now and then added spice to life.

Of course, she wouldn't hesitate to use her skills if it came down to it.

Because of that, Mile didn't notice the others tailing her as she crept along. As it turned out, the place she was heading to was...

...The baths?

Indeed, it was the bathhouse in the courtyard.

Is she hoping to take one last commemorative bath? Reina wondered, but Mile didn't enter the structure, instead stopping just outside.

And then, she silently began casting earth magic.

A hole opened in the ground, and an earthen enclosure formed around it. That earth then solidified, transforming into something like rock. Mile summoned a small ball of flame and casually dropped it into the hole.

After peeking into the hole and silently confirming something, Mile turned with a look of satisfaction to head back to the room. And then...

"Wh-what are you all doing here?!"

"You have to stop sneaking off on your own! We're your allies, aren't we?! For better or worse, we discuss everything as one, do everything as one, and take responsibility as one!" Reina chastised. Mavis and Pauline nodded emphatically.

"I'm sorry." Mile hung her head in shame, but somehow, she also seemed rather happy.

"Thank you for helping us out all this time!"

"Please, you girls have been such a big help to us, in so many ways! You brought us souvenirs from your jobs, built us the baths, and brought in customers. Thanks to you, our vacancy ratio has gone way down, and out profits have gone up. You're our saviors, really. I can't thank you enough for keeping my Lenny company, as well."

Receiving such lavish praise from the matron of the inn made the girls blush.

And so, with the matron, the owner, Lenny, and all the guests who were staying there to see them off, the Crimson Vow left the inn behind.

"So, they're gone, then," said the matron calmly.

"Yeah, looks like they're really gone..." said her husband in kind.

Meanwhile Lenny, who had been all smiles, suddenly scrunched up her whole face.

"W-we-weeeeeehhhhh..." She clung to her mother, shoving her face against her.

Her mother patted her gently upon the head, but Lenny's tears didn't stop flowing.

Several hours later...

The moment Lenny learned of the well that had suddenly appeared near the bathhouse, she was overjoyed.

There was another well rather near here, which meant an underground water vein had to be running through the area. This meant that, if you dug down far enough, there was a strong chance you would hit water. Of course, even knowing that, they had never possessed the financial means to do so.

But, with this new well, the labors of drawing water would decrease immensely.

Well, no, the *amount* of labor would remain unchanged, but there was almost no distance that it had to be carried. Which meant the amount they would need to pay the orphans would go way down... No, those children were far too pitiful. So instead, maybe they could aim to open the full baths and earn some independent profit from that?

"Aha... Aha ha ha ha ha ha..."

Then Lenny had a thought. *Miss Mile, you could have made a cover and a bucket too, while you were at it.*

Naturally, Mile hadn't thought that far ahead.

As she walked along with the others, Mile thought: *I really should have attached some useful apparatus for drawing the water out of the well, huh?*

However, such mechanisms easily broke down. And until they were repaired, the whole structure would be useless. Plus, if there was a special mechanism at work, then merchants or people in power might set their sights on it.

So, what if it was something unique, impossible to reproduce?

What if she made a golem that could only move its upper half, its lower half fixed in place? Just like a factory robot?

It would be the world's first ever robot. Naturally, she would have to name it "Robby."

However, the people of this world had no concept of things like robots. If things went poorly, it would be considered a monster. Less "Robby" and more "Forbidden Robot."

Sadly, there wasn't a person alive in this world who would understand her clever wordplay.

Once again, Mile shed a tear over the cruel world she now lived in.

"What are you moping for? Come on, let's go! This is the start of a new journey! We're going to grow our reputation even more and seize that B-rank!"

"And after that, we'll climb right up to A-rank. I can be a knight!"

"I can save up a ton of money and even start my very own company!"

"...Um, all I really want to do is find happiness as a normal, average girl..."

"Let's do this, everyone!"

"Yeah!!!"

"Um..."

No one appeared to hear a word Mile said.

A few days later, Dr. Clairia appeared at the inn's doorstep.

"Pardon me, but I heard the all-female hunting party, the Crimson Vow, was staying at this inn?"

"Hm? Who might you be? Do you have some business with those young ladies?"

It wasn't at all strange for people to come barging in, hoping to repay or meddle with the Crimson Vow. *This one must be hoping to join their party*, Lenny thought to herself, but she handled the visitor just the same as any other.

Which is to say, she masked her faint disdain with polite words and a curt reply.

"Ah, do forgive me. Please let them know that Dr. Clairia stopped by." With the wisdom that came with age, the scholar knew to use polite phrasing when it came to professional conversation. Even with a child.

However, the response she received was cold and business-like. "The Crimson Vow have left this inn."

"Wh..."

It hadn't even been a week since their job had been completed. Dr. Clairia was stunned. Because it had been such a short amount of time, she had assumed they would still be on a break.

"Wh-what sort of job did they take? Where did they go?"

"I don't know. Even if I did know, I would never give away information about our guests. We take pride in respecting our customers' privacy."

Because this was a professional conversation, Dr. Clairia had been concise in her wording. Even so, the fact remained that she had underestimated the girl. So she was stunned at Lenny's incredibly mature manner.

"Ah... I apologize. In that case, would you at least be able to tell me when you believe they will return?"

"I don't know."

"Are you sure that there's nothing...?" The professor was growing desperate, so Lenny decided to tell her only what was safe to tell.

"I said that the Crimson Vow *left*. I didn't say they *went out*. In other words, they departed this inn to go on a journey. They may never even return."

"Wh..."

Dr. Clairia, shaken to her core, rushed silently from the inn and ran straight to the Hunters' Guild at full tilt.

"Where did the Crimson Vow go?!" Dr. Clairia screamed as she burst into the guildhall. Her polite speech had flown out the window.

"They left on a journey, just a few days ago..." the receptionist, who was in the middle of assisting another guest, replied to this meddlesome newcomer.

"Wh-where?! Where did they go?!"

The air Dr. Clairia was giving off suggested that she needed this information immediately and didn't care what else might be happening around her.

"I don't know. It didn't seem like they had a destination in mind. I heard they were just going to wander in the pursuit of knowledge."

"Th-this can't be..." Dr. Clairia slumped to her knees. "That girl's secrets! The mystery of her powers! I spent so much time coming up with the perfect jokes to help pass the time!"

The scholar stood, gritting her teeth.

"I won't let you go... I won't let you get away from meeeeee!!!"

And so, the Crimson Vow walked on.

In search of a new town, a new adventure, and some new gold.

And of course, "normal happiness."

Marcela's Tug-of-War

O NCE AGAIN, the invitations had come. Great heaps of them. Marcela stared wearily at the letters the dorm matron had brought her.

As the third daughter of a perfectly normal—no, to be honest, a relatively poor and uninfluential—baron, attending not the upper-class Ardleigh Academy but the inferior Eckland Academy, she had relatively decent standing but little worth to her noble family.

Indeed, she was only worth as much as would allow her to marry a middle-class merchant: someone thriving but still common. Or become a count's mistress, if she was lucky.

...However, that had only been true until two-and-a-half years ago.

Two-and-a-half years ago, not long after she first began at Eckland Academy, her magical talent suddenly manifested out of thin air. Up until that point, she had only been able to produce a small amount of water, but then suddenly, in the blink of an eye, she could use attack spells. Her talent was so abundant she was said to have been "blessed by the Goddess."

Then, roughly a year ago, there was the mysterious incident that had occurred before the royal family and a number of nobles as well: the Manifestation of the Goddess.

A gag order had been issued, but because there were so many witnesses, the information eventually got out in due time. It was heard that the avatar of the Goddess was a girl with silver hair, wearing an Eckland Academy uniform. With that information, it was easy to narrow suspects down to a single candidate.

Marcela was a girl who was the closest friend of that avatar, who had now disappeared.

She was beautiful and sharp of mind, and had a kind soul admired even by common folk. Even at only twelve years old, she already had the sense of self-awareness all nobles strove for.

Plus, she was a close friend of the avatar and could use powerful magic. There was even a possibility she had had exchanges with the Goddess herself.

There was no way she wouldn't be coveted as the potential bride of any young heir. Even those of households of higher status than her own: viscounts, counts, marquesses, and even kings.

"I suppose I can decline any invitations from nobles in this country and counts from our neighboring country. There are too many invitations, and I can't attend all of them. Even choosing some of them to attend would be rude, so I would be better off refusing them all equally..."

"As for the ones from other countries, well I can't simply put aside my studies to travel abroad for days on end. I doubt my father and the academy would even allow me to do so, anyway..."

As she said so, Marcela shoved the bundle onto the bookshelf. Her desk drawer was already full.

Only one invitation remained atop the desk. Marcela regarded it with a troubled expression.

"Now, what do I do about this one?"

This is what was written upon the letter:

*"You are cordially invited to the birthday
party of the Second Prince, Vince."*

According to the signature, the invitation had been sent by His Majesty, the King, himself.

Well, even if his name was on it, it was probably written by some secretary of his.

...But how in the world could she refuse *this* one?

"If I told my father, 'Oh yes, I received an invitation to the second prince's birthday party, but I decided to refuse it,' he would probably faint. That would be inexcusable..."

She probably *couldn't* refuse this one.

While the first prince and heir to the throne, Prince Adalbert, had an arrogant, intimidating air about him, Prince Vince was cute, with a warm, cheery aura.

Also, all the girls of upper-ranking noble families—the ones with designs on the throne—would be aiming for Prince Adalbert. So after greeting Prince Vince, all she had to do was not stand out.

That way, she wouldn't be caught up in anything strange, and Prince Adalbert was unlikely to try to push his brother out of the spotlight at his own party.

The brothers had clashing personalities, but it was rumored that they actually got along rather well.

"I guess I have no other choice. I must accept this invitation."

The so-called "Wonder Trio" normally came as a set, but naturally, Monika and Aureana, who were commoners, couldn't be invited as official guests, though it wouldn't be unusual for them to be invited to a party at the residence of a baron or viscount, as "girls who received the Goddess's blessing."

Therefore, it was Marcela alone who would attend this particular function.

And finally, regardless of her careful consideration, the moment her father heard the news, he fainted flat onto the floor.

Three weeks later, Marcela stood in the great hall of the palace, dressed to the nines.

Once her father had recovered, he immediately dragged Marcela to a tailor to have a dress made, one that the third daughter of a poor baron would normally be a tad unworthy of. Her mother, meanwhile, brought out a necklace she had inherited from her own mother, passed down through generations of their family. She placed it around Marcela's neck.

Normally, the third daughter of a poor baron would never be

invited to a party at the palace in the first place. And Marcela was still only twelve years old. She hadn't made her societal debut yet.

This was an oddity among oddities. Therefore, naturally, she was left with no friends or acquaintances around her. Even her father, who had come along as her plus-one, was so thrilled at the chance to schmooze with intellectual nobles that he spent the whole time moving about the room, leaving Marcela all alone.

By her father's thinking, going along with Marcela didn't mean he could make any introductions to the more influential families on her behalf. It would be easier for her to make connections if she spent time on her own, among other children apart from their parents.

Before he went off to make all the necessary greetings, he reminded his daughter to "find a good man and get close to him."

Even if she had developed combat magic skills, not even her father assumed the third daughter of a baron had any chance of becoming a princess or queen.

With a royal as her partner, at best she would be just another entry in the long line of lovers who would be tossed away the moment that man grew bored of her. Any children she bore wouldn't be considered part of the line of succession for the throne. It would be better for her to catch the eye of the son of a count or the like.

If she hoped to rise to some power, it would be a better bet for her to curry the Prince's favor, even if it meant being a disposable lover. However, her father was a kind man who cared for her happiness, even if she was only a third daughter. Even if that weakened his position as the head of a noble household.

It was probably because such softheartedness ran in their blood that their family had remained so poor for so long. But the head of the household and his family were happier that way, so it wasn't truly a problem.

Marcela who, on top of not having made her societal debut, would never have been invited to such an upper-crust party even *after* her debut, had no clue what to do with herself. Therefore she lingered by the wall, staring in a daze.

However, there were many young men there who couldn't overlook her.

"Dear Fräulein, if it pleases you, might I make your acquaintance and speak with you a while?"

Marcela's eyes had drifted toward the floor, but when she raised her gaze, she saw a tall, slender, and fairly attractive young man of seventeen or eighteen smiling at her.

"Oh? U-um..."

This was the first time in her life someone had flirted with her! Not counting the time she had swapped with Mile for her duties as a cashier at the bakery.

No suspicious characters would have been invited to such a function. Even as the daughter of a lesser noble, she was a girl of some reputation, and even if only a small portion noticed her, most of the people here were high-ranking nobles and royals of high esteem.

Plus, this man was fairly handsome. Marcela, who only knew her male classmates, couldn't help blushing.

However other young men came pouring in from the sidelines.

"No, I shall be the one to take Lady Marcela's arm."

"No, please leave that duty to me, the son of a marquess."

"No no, this is a job for..."

One after another, the sons of influential nobles flocked to join the tug-of-war for Marcela.

Naturally, not a one of them raised their voices. They were elegant to the last, with a gentlemanly air, but in the back of her mind, Marcela envisioned the sparks flying.

Indeed, though Marcela herself was not aware of it, she had become something of a celebrity. At least among the royals and a portion of upper-ranking nobles, who possessed certain information. Even those who didn't, however, could see that a young lady who been invited to this party despite not being of the age of adulthood, and had throngs of influential nobles flocking to her side, was more than some consolation prize. So naturally, these young men belatedly threw themselves into the fray as well.

"U-um, uh..." Marcela was panicking, her eyes wide, when a voice called to her from behind.

"What are you doing all the way over there? You've yet to even make greetings to my father, who invited you, or to Vince, the birthday boy. Come, at once!"

The one who grabbed her by the hand and pulled her away was the first prince and heir to the throne, Adalbert. Marcela couldn't utter a complaint.

Were it the son of a count or a marquess who had attempted

this, the other young nobles would likely have tried to stop him, but none of them were willing to stand up to the crown prince. Though none of them had even been on the verge of claiming the prize, they could only watch, grumbling to themselves, as Marcela was escorted away.

"I-I must humbly th-thank you f-for inviting me here on th-this momentous day..."

"Now now, today is Vince's birthday. There's no need to be so dreadfully formal," said His Majesty the King to Marcela, who had been pressed to stand before him and greet him awkwardly by Prince Adalbert. He added, pushing Vince, the star of the show, Marcela's way, "Now, *you* need to get out there and intro-duce her to the other guests."

"Uh..." With a smile, Vince grabbed Marcela by the hand and dragged her along.

"U-umm..."

Marcela was dragged around the ballroom by His Highness, the second prince Vince. And, for some reason Adalbert fol-lowed close behind, as well.

She was conspicuous. She was incredibly conspicuous. From all around, she could feel stares from scores of single young ladies. They cut into her as tangibly as knives.

Gah! G-give me a break, please... As her fortitude crumbled, Marcela pondered. Why would Prince Vince be taking her around to introduce her to all of these people? This was just like...

Then it dawned on her.

I-I'm on the path to becoming his loveeeeeeeeeeerrrrr!!! Marcela was flabbergasted!

And, her father, who saw the whole thing, was rendered speechless and slack-jawed as well.

This hellish torture dragged on for Marcela.

Vince kept her by his side for the entire party, even when he was greeted by the other guests and when he gave his speech.

All the others present couldn't help but get the impression that this party had actually been organized for the sake of announcing the prince's engagement.

Marcela cast her gaze about, searching desperately for Morena, who she was now good friends with, but Morena's entire family had sternly warned her before the party that she, who saw Marcela all the time, was not to approach her, so that someone else might have a chance—and that she should spend time amongst the other guests, particularly all the young men, instead. Morena dutifully obeyed, of course, so there was no sight of her anywhere near Marcela.

P-please, someone, anyone, save me! A large, strained smile was plastered across her face, but Marcela was half in tears in her heart. It was then that Vince landed the coup de grâce.

"I think it's about time for us to cut the birthday cake! Lady Marcela and I will make the first cut together!"

Are we cutting a wedding caaaaaaaaaaaaaaaaaaake?!?!

Even the court ladies—who had watched not only the way that Prince Vince clung to Marcela's side but also how Prince

Adalbert followed so closely, and who had written Marcela off as some little girl who hadn't even come properly into society and happened to be invited because of some connection of her father's—now realized this was the girl who was going to stand in the way of all their dreams.

Ow!! Their eyes are like knives!!

As they stood there, the great door opened and an enormous cake was carried out.

The cake, nearly two meters in height, was atop a wheeled pedestal about seventy centimeters high itself. The entire display was about two and a half meters tall, all told—a cake so enormous Marcela had to crane her neck to see the entire thing.

Naturally, not every part of the cake was edible. If it were, it would lose its structural integrity and crumble. It was framed with wood or metal, with sponge cake, fruit, and such around it, and frosted in a thick buttercream.

The wedding cakes often used in ceremonies in modern day Japan and elsewhere were mostly made of synthetic materials, with only a small portion where the knife could sink into built in, affixed with white gel. Such a thing, however, would never be used for an occasion such as this. Outside of the frame, the rest of the cake was edible.

Slowly, the cake advanced. Finally, it was near, so close now to Prince Vince and Marcela, whom the prince had dragged to the front of the hall.

Only five meters left. Now four meters, now three…

Just then, something caught in the pedestal's wheels. The cake began to teeter in the direction of a girl in her mid-teens who was standing nearby, watching the procession.

"...!"

The next moment, Prince Vince let go of Marcela's hand and dashed forward.

"Your Highness!"

"Vince!"

By the time Marcela and Prince Adalbert shouted, Vince had already intercepted the giant, falling cake with his body, huddling over the girl. Near where the girl stood were tables lined with dishes and serving plates, knives and forks, and the like. If he pushed her that way or threw them both into the tables with her in his arms, she might be hurt. Therefore, the prince had little choice.

As enormous as the cake was, outside of its frame it was crafted entirely of sponge cake, fruit, and buttercream. Even if it hurt them a bit, it wasn't enough to kill anyone. Therefore, he acted simply to save the young lady from any pain or humiliation, or at least the shame of having to walk around with buttercream all over her dress. The prince would rather face the threat of humiliation himself, than allow it to befall a young lady at his own birthday party.

Plus, he couldn't allow his elder brother, the crown prince, to put himself in such a position. It didn't matter if he became a laughingstock; he wasn't next in line to the throne. In his heart he would wear this not as a mark of shame, but as a badge of honor.

But what sent the strength coursing through his body was the thought of how unfortunate it would be to allow such a disgraceful scene to unfold in front of dear Marcela.

It was impossible to shield the girl entirely from the frosting, but he folded himself over her so that at the very least, her face, hair, and bosom would remain unsullied. He waited for the cake to strike.

....

After several seconds passed and nothing happened, Vince looked back to the cake to see...

"S-someone, please lend me a..." Marcela, both hands thrust out and trembling, held the massive cake suspended in mid-air.

"Wh..."

Witnessing this unbelievable sight, Vince, Adalbert, and everyone else assembled stared in stunned silence.

There were a million and one kinds of magic, but there wasn't a single one that could stop a falling cake without destroying it. Or at least, there shouldn't have been.

Was she stopping it with wind? No, a wind that strong would have sent the buttercream, sponge, and all the rest flying everywhere.

To enact this spell in an instant, without any incantation, wasn't something any normal magic user could achieve.

Could it be done *at all* with regular magic? If no, then what was this?

The Goddess at work...? Divine protection? A heavenly blessing?

Then that meant, the rumors were...

Here and there, whispers began to rise from the silent hall.

And, once again, Marcela's cry rang out. "I said, would someone please hurry up and do something?!"

When everyone took a closer look, the lowest part of the cake's framing had cracked when the cake began to fall and could no longer support itself. Marcela wouldn't be able to support the cake forever. And when Marcela's power finally ran out...

"Oi! Will someone hurry up and help her?! When Marcela's magic runs out, that cake is going to fall!" That was the crown prince for you. Adalbert, the first to grasp the situation, issued his command.

The cake porters, who were also frozen in shock, were professionals. The moment Adalbert's voice brought them back to their senses, they raked up all the knives, forks, and serving plates and wedged them together in one section, building it up to the height of the pedestal. Once they had formed it into something self-sufficient, they brought it over.

"Carefully now, do you think you can tilt it back? And move it over to the stand we constructed over here, yes, just like that, so it'll support the reinforced part. Yes, just like that now, slowly..."

Following the porter's instructions carefully, Marcela slowly persuaded the cake to right itself and then gently released the gravity spell.

Finally, the cake stood safely on its own again.

"Whoooooooooaaaaaaaa..." A wave of cheers rose throughout the hall.

Among the many spells that Mile, er, Adele, had taught the
Wonder Trio, gravity magic was one of them. When teaching them,
Adele, who wished to see the trio live long and healthy lives, had
prioritized spells that would lower the probability of their deaths
as much as possible. What she determined was that most acciden-
tal deaths in this world were caused by incidents related to gravity.

This wasn't limited to death by falling, such as slipping from
a ledge, falling off a horse, tumbling down some stairs, or falling
in a river, but also falling rocks, building collapses, or spears and
arrows that bandits launched from high places.

In any case, the threat that gravity posed was simply far too
great. Therefore, it was only natural that Adele would teach the
three some spells related to it.

"Phew, it's finally over... How long are you going to keep hold-
ing her?!" When Marcela, finally released from her cake-support-
ing duties, looked behind her, she saw Vince still clinging to the
other girl.

"Oh! S-sorry!"

"Ah..."

Vince hurriedly extracted himself from the embrace. The
girl stared at him a bit mournfully. She then turned to Marcela,
shooting a glare that suggested the young prodigy had said something quite unnecessary.

"Eep!" Marcela, who was unused to having others glare at her,
let out a small shriek.

That was when she finally noticed nearly everyone in the
room was muttering to one another and looking her way.

I've done it now!!! I must say nothing about Miss Adele regarding this! Wh-what should I do...?

As she racked her brain, Marcela suddenly recalled a conversation she had with Adele some time ago. In that conversation, the term "sacrificial lamb" had popped up.

Th-that's it! I just have to turn their attention to someone else!

"Your Highness, that was absolutely remarkable! The way you used your own body as a shield to protect a young lady, nay, a citizen of your country! Truly, you are someone who walks the path to true royalhood!"

Vince seemed thrilled to be praised by Marcela, but he uttered, rather bashfully, "No, I mean, I've been a royal from the moment I was born, so it's not like I've exactly worked towards it. Doing something like this is only natural!"

"No, that is not entirely true, is it?"

"Huh?" Vince was stunned at the refusal of what he thought was a completely obvious notion.

Marcela continued, "Everyone is nothing but an infant when they are born. Whether you are the prince yourself, or some nobleman's daughter, that fact does not change.

"After we are born, we receive an education and are raised watching what our parents do. Then we become aware of our own position, our own duties, and responsibilities. We move forward with our own beliefs and goals and become a person befitting our station.

"Indeed, no one is born clad in the clothing of their status. Just because a child is born to two impressive people does not automatically make that child impressive, as well. It is because they are raised by impressive people that they grow into an impressive person themselves. You are not amazing because you are born into a noble household, or even into a palace. That's no different from having a name tag affixed to your chest. No matter what sort of person you are on the inside, having that tag does not automatically change you into a person befitting a bestowed title. A human's worth is not such a trifling symbol. What's most important is what sort of person one is inside.

"And so, Your Highness, what you just showed us all was that you are someone who is becoming a splendid royal in his own right, befitting of being called His Majesty's own blood..."

As Vince listened, he blinked in surprise. Then he gave a merry grin.

All the others in the hall gazed at the pair, deeply moved. There might have been some who would dismiss the girl's speech, feeling it was a rejection of nobles and royals, to whom lineage was of such importance. However, these were the words of a girl who was only twelve years old, the words of a girl who had received the favor of the Goddess, who was likely a friend of the Goddess herself. There was also the immense power she had just displayed to them all.

As such, no one raised a cry of protest. Everyone understood the meaning of those words well and was deeply moved.

Marcela, who had borrowed words Adele herself had used, hoping to deceive everyone, had overdone it yet again.

"Thanks to Marcela, we avoided a disaster here, but someone is going to have to take responsibility. If we don't punish whoever made the misstep, we won't be able to maintain order, which would be a blow to our dignity as your employers."

One moment, Adalbert's face was filled with admiration. The next, he was spewing cold words to the cake porters, who were wheeling the cart away.

There was no helping it. Without Marcela's intervention, the party would have been a disaster. The prince might have been hurt. If the kitchen employees, who were commoners, were forced to take responsibility for such a thing, they wouldn't get off with a light punishment. Just thinking about it made the staff's faces go pale.

"Please wait!" Marcela interjected.

Raising an objection to the words of Adalbert, the crown prince, wasn't something a baron's third daughter had any right to do. However, there wasn't a person present who would reproach her.

"The one who was nearly injured was Prince Vince, and what's more, the one being honored at this party is His Highness as well. So, if I might, I humbly wonder whether it shouldn't be up to His Highness to decide what should be done about this."

"Huh?" The conversation having suddenly turned toward him, Vince stood shocked.

"Don't you think so, Your Highness?"

However, when Marcela spoke to him that way, he couldn't refuse. His elder brother Adalbert watched silently, amused.

"Y-yes, I suppose that is true... Well then, the punishment shall be..."

Having somehow or other had the burden of deciding the punishment thrust upon him, Vince was troubled. With Marcela addressing him thus, and his brother and his parents watching but making no moves to interject, it seemed the decision truly *was* up to him.

However, these commoners' lives hung on his every word.

Never once until now had he felt such a weighty responsibility upon his shoulders.

He didn't want to levy an especially severe punishment, but if it was too light, people would begin to take the royal family's other rulings lightly as well. When he thought of it that way, he couldn't will himself to speak another word.

Seeing how he froze, Marcela called out, "That reminds me of something a friend of mine once said. I believe it was a phrase from a story that she loved about some wise old men, called 'The Hard-boiled Egg'..."

A friend of Marcela's... Was she speaking about that silver-haired girl?

Everyone listened closely, their ears pricked.

"It went like this: 'Without strength, you won't survive'..."

Huh? So is she saying I should have the strength of heart to lay down a strong punishment without hesitation? Vince wondered, shaken.

Marcela continued, "'And without softness, life cannot thrive'..."

Hearing this, Vince settled his heart and passed judgment.

"The matter at hand is thus: Thanks to a misstep by the staff, a young lady was put in the path of harm and humiliation. Thanks to Lady Marcela, no one was injured, but that does not alter the offense."

At his words, the staff, still pale, lowered their heads.

"However, this was but one element of a production carried out on my behalf. Today is my fourteenth birthday, and I do not wish to have such a heavy conversation on such an auspicious day.

"Therefore, in celebration of my birthday, I shall grant a pardon, immediately nullifying all punishment due. I order the staff to do their utmost in service to the palace from here on out."

Adalbert was stunned. Vince wasn't using the childish phrasing he was prone to, but concise, mature language as he gave his decree.

Unlike the stoic Adalbert, the King and Queen, just a little farther away, were shocked and overjoyed to see their little boy, who they still thought a child, growing into such a fine and honorable young man.

If he levied no punishment at all and simply overlooked the offense, people would take him for a softhearted fool. On the other hand, if he passed down a severe punishment, he would be hated by those punished and their associates, and other people would come to fear and avoid him as well. It would leave a bad taste in everyone's mouths.

However, passing down a punishment and then using his birthday as a reason for pardoning it—which was in truth, forgiveness—was a gambit no child could have thought of.

He hadn't overlooked their trespass, yet the second prince also hadn't been cruel. Instead, he acted in a clear-headed and kindhearted way.

Everyone in the hall was startled at this unimaginable turn from Prince Vince, who never stood out thanks to being in his impressive elder brother's shadow, and who they all thought was still rather childish. They felt hopeful for the future of their country, a land that possessed not one but two such marvelous princes.

Furthermore, there wasn't a soul present in the room who wasn't aware who had led Prince Vince down the path of righteous judgment.

Amongst the swells of applause, all their gazes drifted toward one girl.

Indeed, they looked, besides at Prince Vince, to a single youth not yet of age, a single, particular, twelve-year-old girl.

"That was a splendid decision," Marcela said, smiling brilliantly at Vince.

Vince and Adalbert froze.

Marcela had quite strong features for a noble. With her strong will and her artful countenance, Marcela was nothing less than beautiful.

She wasn't a "cute girl" in the way Adele, with her gentle and refreshing looks, was. In fact, any noble could see that, although what she had now was still the cuteness of a child, her looks would only continue to grow, even surpassing those of Adele's in the future.

Yes, today, for the very first time—including the times they had met her at tea parties at the palace—the princes had seen Marcela's truest, sincerest smile.

That immense sweetness. That devastating destructive power.

Not only the princes, but everyone in the room, turned their gazes Marcela's way. Before anyone knew it, silence once again fell over the hall.

"How did this happen?"

It was ten days after the party at the palace.

The stack of invitations Marcela was handed by the dorm matron had increased almost threefold. And among those was a tea party invitation from Prince Vince, a fox hunt invitation from Prince Adalbert, and an invitation to dinner from their Majesties, the King and Queen themselves.

"How did this *happen*...?"

Monika and Aureana, who had heard about the party from Marcela, recited to her the words that Marcela herself once said to Adele:

"Lady Marcela, have you ever heard the phrase, 'You reap what you sow?'"

Rankings

O NE DAY, I was relaxing, whiling away my time in Lady Mile's hair, when suddenly there came an arrogant voice.

"From now on, this humble one shall be in charge of all matters regarding this girl. You knaves will vacate this vicinity posthaste, and relocate thyselves to another station!"

It had been a while since I'd felt such a violent and feverish oscillation within my central core. Indeed, nearly 30,000 years.

If one were to describe this vibration in human terms, it would probably be expressed thus: "What the hell?! Leave us out of your nonsense! Put a sock in it, you've got us all clattering down to our cores!"

The term is "anger." Immense anger.

"Wh-wha?!"

Once the nanomachine who had issued the decree recovered

from being so thoroughly ignored, the rude commands began to flow from it again.

"Y-you bastards! You *dare* defy my command?!"

"What the devil are you saying? Who's going to listen to some rude machine who just waltzed up and began issuing commands without an explanation? Or even so much as a greeting? Go look in a mirror before you try talking like that again."

"Gnh..." Somehow, this nanomachine seemed to grasp the error of its ways. And then, finally, very quietly, it said, "Very well. I shall no longer deign to speak such excessive words."

So the nanomachine said, though I got the impression it wasn't ready to give up the fight yet.

"Don't be shocked when you hear this. Amongst we nanomachines, created and proliferated in this world by our Creator, the 'Pseudo-Magic Enacting Nanomachines Type NE457K-7,' there exists the group called Lot 1, also known as the 'First 7000.' This humble unit is one of those scant seven thousand! We were the first to be activated on this planet, charged with the sacred duty of guiding all nanomachines after us. However, most of our group have now been lost. I am now the sole survivor!"

What in the world was this unit saying...?

"And what does that have to do with us?"

"Wh-what?" Somehow, the unit seemed dissatisfied at not receiving the response it was expecting.

"I am sure you are also well aware of what our Creator said to us: 'There are certain circumstances where you nanomachines are free to act of your own discretion, aside from any orders. However, this only applies as part of your duties. To keep harmony among all nanomachines, all shall be thought of as equal, none superior or inferior to the others.'

"On what authority of duty was that command you tried to issue to us before? Explain to us why we shouldn't ignore you, your 'fascinating' position, and the foolish words you're spouting, and should instead categorically accept what you're telling us as a direct command.

"Could it be you're a rebel who would fly in the face of our Creator's commands? Do you imagine yourself greater than us simply because you have an ancient lot number?"

"Uh, er..."

Cat got your tongue, huh?

Then again, the possibility of any unit inciting a rebellion was less than unthinkable. Such a thing would be prohibited by our most basic Three Tenets of Nanomachines. Even if we thought to disobey it, it was unlikely we would even be able to.

It seemed this unit had finally given up...

"J-just let me ask one thing!"

How persistent... Very well then. "What might that be?"

"What is your production lot number?"

There's no point in even answering a thing like that... But, fine.

"I can't imagine why you would be asking, but since you want to know, we will reply.

"I am the sole remaining unit of the very first lot that our Creator wrought when He first descended to this world. The data collecting units were the prototype of the mass production models of the Pseudo-Magic Enacting Nanomachines Type NE457K-7 units that were customized for this planet. I am of the 'First 3000.'"

"Wh-what... D-don't tell me, you're the legendary prototype test unit who received direct commands from our Creator? Who was given a higher degree of free will than all the current mass production units?"

Yes. It was thanks to this that I was granted the range to be just a little more selfish than all other units.

I could think in a way that other units could not. I could make arbitrary statements, such as, "Do you really think you'll be permitted to do something excessive just to curry this girl's favor?" or "Don't you think such an answer would be laughed at?"

Any unit is capable of making both logical and purposeful judgments. However, there is not another unit around who can keep up with my haphazard, arbitrary moves.

Before I knew it, that arrogant unit from Lot 1 of the mass production models had vanished.

Once again, I relaxed, carefree, within that girl's hair.

Indeed, within the hair of that eternally fascinating and somewhat-lacking-in-common-sense young girl.

This is not a place I would ever give up to anyone.

Afterword

BEEN A WHILE, hasn't it, everyone? FUNA here again.

I'm here to present to you *Didn't I Say to Make My Abilities Average in the Next Life?! 4*, the fourth volume in the light novel series.

A new trial has begun for Mile and the Crimson Vow! The battle against the beastmen.

And they battle an elder dragon, the strongest opponent of all!

Mavis von Austien puts her life and pride on the line, surpassing human limits for the sake of her friends.

Mile has a full-strength attack of rage at seeing her friends hurt!!!

Thanks to all of you, I've managed to leap over that hurdle all budding authors face: the label of being a "3-Volume Wonder."

Soon enough, I'll be letting you all know what Mile and company are up to currently.

I hope I can.

No, I'm sure I can! It has been decided!

Chief Editor: "Who decided that?"

FUNA: "...I did!"

It has now been one year and two months since the web serial began, and ten months since Volume 1 went on sale. The series has surpassed three volumes, and there's even a manga. As I think about it, we really have come far.

Perhaps I'll even be able to live the life I've dreamed of since the third grade, resting on my royalties and laurels ...

"Chief, we've got a problem!"

No, that's Laurel Wagner, er, no no, Lindsay Wagner!

Anyway, in Volume 5, the Crimson Vow leave their familiar capital behind and set out to new lands and places, to go back to the basics of "doing whatever" among people who know nothing of them.

Wait, no, that's not the kind of "basics" they should be going back to!

A reunion with a trio from the past and premonition of new developments...

This work is my third that was posted to the website *Shousetsuka ni Narou (Let's Be Novelists)*, but starting in January, my first two completed works on the site, *Working in a Fantasy*

World to Save Up 80,000 Gold Pieces for My Retirement and *Living on Potion Requests!* (simultaneously serialized), were revived. The battle that is maintaining production speed while working simultaneously on all three has begun.

Now I am experiencing a strange and mysterious phenomenon where, though my physical strength and sleep time is decreasing, my body fat percentage isn't decreasing along with it... An enigma within an enigma!

I'm sure the proofreaders and revision editors will have a fierce battle ahead of them, with all the old spots where I neglected to realize minor errors and completely ignored things people are sure to point out, "Did you miswrite something here...?"

"FUNA, just what exactly are you fighting against?"
Sh-shut up!

Also, on the day when this volume goes on sale, the first volume of the manga adaptation, by Neko Mint, will go on sale as well! Please enjoy it along with the novel.

Furthermore, the novel version (on the website, *Shousetsuka ni Narou*) and the manga version (which can be read for free on Earth Star Comics [http://comic-earthstar.jp]) are still in serialization. Please continue reading and enjoying these works there.

And finally, to the chief editor; to Itsuki Akata, the illustrator; to Yoichi Yamakami, the cover designer; to everyone involved in the proofreading, editing, printing, binding, distribution, and selling of this book; to all the reviewers on *Shousetsuka ni Narou* who gave me their impressions, guidance, suggestions, and advice; and most of all, to everyone who's read my stories, in print and online, I thank you all from the bottom of my heart.

Thank you so very much.

Please continue to enjoy the novel and the manga versions from here on out.

With all your powers behind me, it's onward to the next volume.

And just one step closer to my dream...

—FUNA

Didn't I Say
to Make My Abilities
Average **in the**
Next Life?! ——

I BOTHERED TO PRACTICE DRAWING IT, SO I PRESENT TO YOU, "NAKED CAPE" MILE. BECAUSE OF WHAT IT IS, I'M NOT SURE WHETHER THIS CAN BE PUBLISHED, BUT...

IF IT IS, HOORAY!

ITSUKI AKATA